Louis A. Priolo

AS FOR ME AND MY HOUSE

Whitaker House

PITTSBURGH and COLFAX STS., SPRINGDALE, PA 15144

© 1976 by Whitaker House
Printed in the United States of America
ISBN 0-88368-077-7
All Rights Reserved

Whitaker House
Pittsburgh and Colfax Streets
Springdale, Pennsylvania 15144

Some of the names in this book have been changed to protect the individuals involved. The events are as described.

All Scripture passages, unless otherwise indentified, are from *The New American Standard Bible,* used by permission of The Lockman Foundation © 1971, La Habra, California. Quotations from *The Living Bible* used by permission of Tyndale House © 1971, Wheaton, Illinois.

Dedicated with love
> to my wife, Dottie, and my five children—Pam, Jim, Gail, Gina, and Shelley—for their perseverance through our many years of trials; and to Sav Pasqualucci, who through much patience and compassion became highly instrumental in bringing peace to me and my family.

Acknowledgement is given
> to Glenn Cowher for his encouragement during the writing of this book and for his kind help in editing it,
> and
> to my daughter, Gina, for her tremendous help in the task of typing the manuscript.

Contents

Chapter 1

THE CRISIS

I had reached the end of my rope. My whole world was crashing in on me. To even walk through the door of my home caused the ever-present knots in my stomach to tighten painfully. My five children were growing more discontented and rebellious with each passing day; my only son, recently discharged from the Navy, was caught in the snare of drug addiction; my wife, despairing over the chaos in our home, looked to me for answers that I was unable to give.

I had tried so hard to be successful in every area of my life; providing for my family; fighting to reach the top in the field of engineering; struggling to uphold fading morals in a fast-moving world. But, where had it all led? Of what use were all my efforts now?

It was the last day of another painful year. I searched wearily for the possible New Year's resolutions that might free us from our nightmare. But nothing came to mind.

Reflecting back through the fifty-one years of my life, I

tried to find some clue as to where it all began. In the early years I had so much going for me. It seemed that success was certain. I was so confident in my own ability.

My own ability? Well, wasn't the caption in my high school year book an indication of how well I would make it in the future? Didn't it foretell of worldly success? "Louis is one of the few boys who has been outstanding in both athletics and in studies," it read. "A member of the swimming and wrestling teams (simultaneously) and a high honor student to boot. He achieved that distinction even while carrying an exceedingly heavy schedule." I was sure I couldn't lose.

Four years later, I received a Bachelor of Science degree in Metallurgical Engineering from Lehigh University. It was 1941. I could see the signs of World War II coming over the horizon. The pressure was on to join one of the services so I postponed my move into industry and joined the Army Air Forces. At the end of the war, I was discharged as a Major and returned to civilian status, anxious to make my mark in life.

Over the years, my family grew to five healthy and beautiful children. We managed through the mini-tragedies of broken bones, accidents, and occasional illnesses. But those weren't the real problems. If anything, they were the times when we were closest.

Many years went by. I was now an engineering supervisor in a large electronics manufacturing firm. My job covered work in the new technologies of the electronics field. I published several articles and co-authored a book. I traveled to many campuses throughout the country on speaking engagements discussing the newest developments in my work.

I really had career satisfaction. But when my work was done, I had to face the most important area of my life, my family, where I was rapidly losing my grip. The tension was severe. I dreaded going home. So often when I opened the front door, I felt as though I stood face to face with some ominous force. The effect was so overpowering that it took all the courage I could muster to keep from turning around and running, as if to escape this threatening power.

Although on the outside I was moderately successful, on the inside I was a failure, sheltering a dying spirit that was slowly, but surely, strangling me. It was a real paradox. When I first got married I felt that I was ready to lick the world. "I would have a happy family," I thought, "lots of love, lots of togetherness and lots of happiness." There was no question about it. It would happen.

But I had hardly begun married life when my goal started to elude me and my family life began to erode. Each passing year brought increasing difficulties in my relationship with my wife and children. There was a growing communication gap, rebellion, run-away children, drugs, talk about divorce. Each year I would repeatedly conjecture that the next year would be better. But it never was. On the contrary, it was always worse.

My days were plagued with migraine headaches. Even my nights took their toll, repeatedly interrupted by fear-filled nightmares that always ended in a series of wild screams. Little did I know that the nightmares were to continue for many years before I would be delivered from them.

My wife, Dottie, and I sought help from a family counselor. It was a complete zero. I read book after book on how to achieve happiness, a sort of do-it-yourself approach, but without success. I delved into the cults and the occults without success, not realizing that they were areas controlled by Satan and only tended to compound the problems. There were times when I sensed that a mysterious force was methodically destroying me and my family, but I was completely helpless to resist it.

My church seemed incapable of offering any help. I felt that it should have. Sure it was doing a fine job in the educational, organizational, and social areas, but when it came to the real gut needs of the struggling individual, it seemed completely sterile. I needed more than a social religion and I began to rebel. My church attendance appeared to be increasingly pointless. I kept going only to "set a good example for the family." But, what a poor example I was. In time, my family started to see through my facade and all church attendance began to falter.

Finally, we gave up the pretense and all church going came to a grinding halt. This didn't solve any problems, but it might have had one advantage. It eliminated the false sense of religious security that I had when I was "fulfilling my duty" every Sunday. The act of going to church kept my conscience very comfortable, but it completely immunized me against any serious relationship with God. The immunity now wore off. I could no longer pretend to use the church to keep me good enough to satisfy God. Now, it was strictly between Him and me—no crutches.

My decline accelerated and was destined soon to reach a critical stage. All my problems came about because I was excluding God from my life, although I didn't know that at the time. My only contact with Him, be it ever so slight, had been my church attendance. When I removed that little bit of God from my life, there was nothing to keep me from sinking to the bottom.

And sink I did. Christmas Day came, a time to be jolly, peace on earth and good will to all men; and I hit bottom. Family problems had now become monstrous. The final crisis triggered by Jim, my only son, sent me into a deep depression. Our relationship had degenerated to zero. Jim and I used to have so much going for us; real togetherness; swimming, hiking, bicycling, weight lifting, Scuba diving. That was when Jim was younger. But now he was fully grown. The togetherness was only a dim memory.

For the past six years, I had watched him going downhill. Every attempt I made to help him ended in failure. He was now so deeply involved in drugs that he was losing all control of his free will. Bit by bit, my heart was breaking as I watched him deliberately racing down his own path of self-destruction. To make matters worse, several years earlier, he had said, as if prophetically, "I won't live past the age of 22." He was now 22.

One week later, New Year's Day, my entire family was gathered for dinner. I sat down to say grace. My desire to struggle was gone. I felt I could no longer go on and essentially gave up all hope, entertaining thoughts of suicide. But at that moment, a flicker of light suddenly seemed to penetrate this dark hour—a light from God. Was this a ray of hope that by some miracle I could be rescued by God? I had never really considered Him for real help before. He always seemed so far away and my prayers to Him seemed to bounce off the walls. Would He really hear me this time? It was worth trying. Yes, I'll hold out for just one more year.

So it was that in this state of despair and surrender, I grasped this one last hope and cried out, "*Dear Lord, please bring peace to me and my family this year.*" A simple, but desperate prayer; a dozen words to overcome a lifetime of failures, a lifetime of needs.

But who was this God that I cried out to? I knew so little about Him.

As I look back to that painful day, it seems difficult to believe that I could have lived for over half a century and still missed the most important issue of my life, my relationship with God. And yet, that's just what I did. For 51 years I lived without knowing Him, that is not knowing Him personally. I never experienced His presence nor did I believe that anyone really could.

Don't misunderstand me. I had always believed in God, but my God was way out there somewhere, so distant that I was sure He couldn't care what I was doing, much less become involved with my personal life. For someone to suggest this kind of personal God bordered on fanaticism, I thought. I resigned myself to being a "good" Christian, good in my *own* eyes. I went to church on Sundays and religious holidays and took part in the usual religious rituals and ceremonies. But, my God remained infinitely distant and never, to my knowledge, became an active part of my life. My useful knowledge of Him and His activities was essentially zero.

How often, in church, I repeated the Apostle's Creed: "I believe in God, the Father Almighty, Creator of heaven and earth, and In Jesus Christ, His only Son our Lord... I believe in the Holy Ghost..." I believe, I believe, I believe. How phony I was. I did not believe. I was simply repeating memorized words because it was part of the ceremony of the service.

So what *did* I believe? Sure there was a Father God. I always believed that, but I had a lot of trouble with Jesus Christ being His only Son. And the Holy Ghost lost me completely. In spite of that, I continued like a robot, mechanically praying the Creed and hoping that some day when I got older things would clear up.

I got older, but things did not clear up. Instead, I became less and less satisfied with my set of beliefs, which were quickly becoming a set of *unbeliefs*. I searched for answers about God, but found none. I questioned my friends, but they were either as unknowledgeable as I was or else they weren't interested in discussing the subject. A few tried to explain with abstract ideas that were completely hollow and left me even more confused. Mostly, everyone avoided the subject because, "Friends just don't talk about religion. It may cause hard feelings."

Fortunately, even though I did not know God, He knew me, and blessed me and my family and my career in many ways, although I didn't know it at the time. Now, as I look back, I'm sure that God gave me those blessings *on credit* knowing that someday I would see the light and thank Him for them. And I have, many times over. But at the time, I assumed that the blessings were the result of my own ability, with perhaps a little luck thrown in here and there.

But now, on that particular New Year's Day, as I prayed for peace for my family, I was at the point of desperation. Every method that the world had to offer to help me had failed. I was calling out to the only source that I knew was left. My heart cried out to God for help and for many nights following I repeated that prayer at the dinner table, day after day, week after week, month after month. The family soon became accustomed to hearing it. They listened without comment. They knew that I was dead serious. And they knew how much we needed peace. But, they didn't know how it would come. Neither did I. But, we all had hope that it *would* come—somehow.

Unknown to me, God was setting up a plan to answer my plea. It started to unravel in April of that year. I was at my desk during the mid-morning when I became jittery and just had to walk around. I went out into the shop area where I met Sav, a friend who worked for me at one time and whom I hadn't seen for a number of weeks.

We went through the usual greetings. Then he asked with much hesitation, "Lou, would you be interested in going on a Christian retreat this coming weekend?" I said, "A retreat?" and burst out laughing. "Sav, you've got to be kidding. I've given up on religion. In fact, I'm so fed up with religion that I quit going to church entirely. A retreat would be the last thing that I would be interested in." I was sure my answer was quite clear and that our discussion was over so I began to walk away.

But what I didn't know, was that Sav was being used by God. He had been trying for months to get someone to go on this retreat without much success. However, just the previous night, Sav prayed with a friend, asking God to send someone to him whom he could talk to about going. He now felt that I might be that person. The more we talked the more certain he felt about it.

I couldn't shake him free and I became increasingly uneasy as we seemed to be debating the issue. Finally, I thought that I had the clincher that would put the argument to rest. In my rebellion against the church, I refused to pray any of the prayers that I had been previously taught to use in talking to God. I said determinedly, "Listen, Sav, let me try to clarify the picture. I told you I've completely broken my ties with the church, but apparently you don't believe me. The fact is that even when I say grace, or pray at all, I pray entirely in my own words." Since the tradition of our church called for memorized prayer, I was certain that this "shocking confession" would surely end the discussion.

Little did I know that this was a special Spirit-led retreat. It was a three-day weekend of teachings, mainly by laymen, that emphasized a personal relationship with Jesus Christ. A big part of this emphasis was on talking to Him in your own words. Therefore, when I said that I prayed in my own words, instead of defeating Sav, I refueled his engine.

As the discussion continued, I felt that I was losing the

argument so I broke away by saying, "I'll think it over and call you tomorrow." I never intended to do so and expected to forget about the whole thing as soon as I left him. Then Sav made one parting remark, "OK. We'll leave it up to the Lord."

"Leave it up to the Lord? What's the matter with this guy? Is he a fanatic," I wondered, "mentioning the Lord here in work? Besides I'm the one who's making the decision not the Lord." As I walked away I thought, "How ridiculous, me going on a Christian retreat."

But I couldn't seem to get the subject out of my mind. It kept churning over and over. I battled with myself all that day and the next. I definitely didn't want to go! My going on a retreat defied all logic. But something within me refused to accept that logic.

Sav wasn't taking any chances. The next night he called me on the phone to get my answer. By now I didn't seem to have any arguments left. I made one last feeble attempt to resist. As if to propose a conditional agreement, I said, "Sav, I don't want to get trapped into any commitments. No tricks like trying to get me into church through some side door." After that statement, I agreed to go, barely meeting the deadline, since the retreat was due to start the next day.

The weekend program was well-planned covering some fifteen topics, teachings, and testimonies about Jesus, given mostly by laymen. This was interwoven with group discussions. As the retreat unraveled, I began to sense a strange feeling within me as if there were a battle going on. I put up my guard. I was afraid to trust anyone. I had to be careful that they didn't trap me into any commitments. I had had my fill of hypocrisy while in the church and wanted no more of it.

But the battle continued. There was something I couldn't put my finger on. I couldn't understand the heavy emphasis on Jesus. Finally, during one of the twenty minute breaks, I rushed up to my room and yelled out to God, "Lord, what is this all about? What are they really trying to tell me? What's all this talk about Jesus mean?" Then tears streamed down my face as I started to sense the presence of God's love, realizing that this team of men loved Jesus Christ so much that they were giving up their time in the hopes that I, too, would somehow learn to love Him.

I went back to the meeting room. My heart began to soften and continued to do so during the balance of the weekend. Sunday evening came. The retreat was essentially over. We met for a final gathering in a large room filled with several hundred people who met to fellowship with us.

We sat in the front of the room. One by one each person in our group stood up to give a brief testimony of his reaction to the retreat. Although I didn't understand it, the presence of God's love was so overpowering that I buried my head in my hands as a big lump came to my throat and tears flooded my eyes. I tried desperately to fight back the tears so that when it was my turn I could speak coherently. A friend of mine, Frank, got up to talk, but just cried and babbled like a baby. I didn't want to do that. I had to get control of myself. I waited.

Finally, everyone else had spoken. I couldn't delay any longer. Thankfully, the lump was gone and the tears had stopped. I stood up, although I wasn't sure what to say. But the words came. As I looked over the crowd, I suddenly knew without a doubt that Jesus Christ was real. I could feel His presence penetrating my entire being. I felt soaked in His love. In this overpowering atmosphere of God's love I knew Jesus had come into my heart and I said, "Tonight, for the first time in my life, I met Jesus."

At that moment, in my heart, I committed my whole life to Jesus Christ. Then I sat down.

So it was that after fighting bitterly all weekend to keep from being trapped into any commitments, I voluntarily, willingly, and with a tremendous desire to do so, committed my whole life to Jesus Christ. Yes, I found peace, the peace that I had been searching for all these years, because I found Jesus, the Prince of Peace.

After the meeting broke up, I walked over to greet Sav. As I looked into his eyes, all I could see was the love of Jesus, and I could no longer fight back the stream of tears that had been building up all evening. I embraced Sav, and wept like a baby and thanked him over and over again.

Chapter 2

MY ONLY SON

I suddenly realized that for the first time in my life I had the ability to pray. In the past I had seldom prayed because I felt that my prayers didn't go anywhere. They seemed to bounce off the walls. For this reason I limited my prayers almost entirely to saying grace. During the retreat, I looked with envy at the men who seemed to pray with such confidence. I yearned for that ability. Now, through a mystery that I could not comprehend, Jesus answered the desire of my heart by giving me that ability and faith to pray with confidence.

With this new gift from God, I started to pray for my son, Jim, because his need for Jesus was most critical. He was now so deep into drugs that it was essentially impossible to communicate with him. He withdrew more and more into a shell of loneliness, helplessness, and frustration. I couldn't help thinking how for twenty-two years I had tried to lead Jim down the right path, but I failed because I was trying to do it by myself. Now I found the missing ingredient—Jesus Christ. There was no doubt in my mind that somehow Jesus would give him the same freedom from oppression that He had given me. I didn't know how yet, but I was sure it would happen.

I asked Sav for help. "Do you know of any activity directed to the young people?" He said, "Sure, there's a Christian Youth Center located in Allentown, Pennsylvania. I'll take you there tomorrow night."

The next day Sav introduced me to a group of young people at the Center. As soon as I saw them, I knew that this was the place for Jim. These men had a look about them that was different from anything that I was accustomed to seeing. They seemed to be full of love and peace, combined with a wholesomeness that I didn't think existed among the young. But it was just too much to expect that Jim would even *consider* joining this group.

Tony, who appeared to be a leader in the Center, mentioned that in less than two weeks there would be a retreat that was structured to lead young men to a personal relationship with Jesus Christ. As he described it, it sounded much like the retreat that I went on, except that it was geared to the young. My problem was how to get Jim to go. It looked utterly impossible in view of the difficulty in communication we had in the past few years. Even if I were able to get him to hold still long enough to listen, based on past history, I knew that I could never convince him to go. He consistently rebelled at any of my suggestions.

I explained my plight to Tony. He hardly blinked an eye, answering with utmost confidence, "Don't worry. We'll take care of it."

In view of the hopelessness of the situation I couldn't understand his confidence and I wondered just what kind of brilliant strategy he would use. I asked, "How will you go about convincing Jim? What do you plan to do?"

"We'll pray for him," he answered nonchalantly.

Pray for him? Just like that! How could they solve a problem as difficult as Jim's by praying? Although I had just learned how to pray, that still sounded like too much. But Tony's confidence had a way of brushing off on me. If he were so sure that prayer would do the trick, perhaps it really would.

My faith and hope grew by leaps and bounds. I prayed for Jim almost continuously. I could just see everything falling into place. By some miracle Jim would go on the retreat. He would find Jesus and peace like I did. I had no idea how this would come about, but still I had complete confidence that somehow it would.

Then, two days later, my hopes were crushed. Jim disappeared. He left home. There was only a brief message that he gave to my daughter, Pam. She said that he told her, "I just have to get away to get things straightened out." There was nothing else. I didn't know where he went or why or for how long.

When will he stop running? I surely thought that by now he would. But it seemed to be a built-in reaction. As soon as things got bad, he ran.

My mind went back as though racing through the pages of a book. It was the last day of his junior year in high school. I was looking at his report card in disbelief. He had always been a good scholar, but now he failed algebra and didn't do too well in the other subjects. It was, in fact, the first time any of my children failed a subject.

I had had high hopes that when Jim graduated from high school, he would go to college and possibly study engineering. But this sudden reversal, this failure in algebra, killed that hope.

This was a new kind of blow. It looked like his chances at college just died.

My temper flared as I told him how serious it was. He sat quietly and listened without commenting. The atmosphere was tense for the entire evening. I went to bed still terribly upset.

At 4:00 A.M. I was suddenly awakened with an uneasy feeling. Somehow I sensed that something was wrong. I went into Jim's bedroom to check on him and found that he was gone. I woke up Dottie. "Quickly, get up," I said, "Jim's gone." We both got dressed and began checking throughout the house. We found that many of his clothes were missing from his closet. I checked the garage and saw his clothing inside the Rambler.

I quickly called to Dottie, "His clothes are in the Rambler so he must still be around here somewhere." I picked up a flashlight and went outside to search the grounds.

As I walked around the back of the house, I saw a silhouette in the shadows at one corner of the house. It was Jim. He was just standing there looking completely lost. It made me feel terribly guilty for having yelled at him. I walked over to him and said, "Jim, why don't you come on inside?" He did.

I learned that he had tried to leave home. However, because of a series of circumstances and a "freak" failure in the car, he came back home. In fact, he had to push the car part way home, a feat of strength that was difficult to comprehend.

The pages continued to flip by—several more attempts to leave home, a hitch in the Navy, involvement in drugs, a court martial, a long series of traffic violations, and heavier drug involvement. The gap between us grew and grew.

Six years had gone by since he first tried to leave home

and now he fled again. But why this time? It didn't follow any of the previous patterns. We had no arguments, no flare-ups. Why did he have to take things into his own hands again just when God was moving in. And now his strain for independence ruined God's plans to get him on the retreat.

The next morning, as I drove to work, I had to struggle in my prayers for Jim because I was in a terrible state of anxiety over his disappearance. I questioned the Lord about this change of events. Suddenly, I seemed to receive a message through an inner voice. Since I was so young in the Lord, I was not aware that God often speaks through an inner voice. Nevertheless, in spite of my ignorance, the message came through with unquestionable clarity.

"*When you ask Me to do something, don't tell Me how to do it.*"

Don't tell God how to do it? Was I limiting God by telling Him how to reach Jim? It took only moments to realize that Jim didn't upset *God's* plans; he upset *my* plans.

Thank You, Lord. Now I understand. My complete trust in God came back. It no longer mattered how the Lord would reach Jim. Retreat or no retreat I would trust Him to do it His way.

As I came to this understanding, a wave of love came into my heart which took away all my previous anxiety. I was now able to resume praying with confidence and continued to do so throughout the following days.

Five days later, a group of us met for a prayer meeting at a church in nearby Allentown. After the formal part of the meeting, Sav and another friend, Denny, joined me to pray for Jim since they both knew of my deep concern for him. We knelt together at the altar and prayed, first Sav, then Denny and finally me. Although neither Sav nor

Denny had ever met Jim, the love of Jesus was so strong in them that they prayed with the same deep compassion that I felt for him.

As we prayed in this atmosphere of concern, I suddenly felt the powerful presence of God. His love grew so strong that it seemed to envelope me and penetrate every cell of my body. At the same time, it felt as though I were being lifted up into the heavens along with Sav and Denny. For some moments, the three of us seemed to blend together, suspended in a unity that I still cannot fathom even to this day. I was so overwhelmed by the presence of God that the tears just poured from my eyes and I felt compelled to embrace Sav and Denny, ignoring any concern about worldly embarrassment.

While I was wrapped in this blanket of love, God assured me that He was taking excellent care of Jim. It was a kind of assurance that everything was working out according to God's plan. He was in full control.

When I got home that night I could still feel the deep presence of Jesus. I wanted to stay close to Him and felt drawn to read about Him in the Bible. Suddenly Scripture seemed to jump out at me as though it were alive, bringing me closer and closer to Jesus. I didn't want to stop. I read on and on soaking up every word until fatigue finally overcame me and I fell into a deep peaceful sleep.

The next day Jim came home. Somehow, deep within my spirit I knew that he would. It was part of the assurance that the Lord had given me the night before. After supper Jim and I sat down in the family room to talk, just the two of us. It was hard to believe we had fallen so far away from each other. But Jim had finally stopped running. Slowly he explained, "I was addicted to heroin— a mainliner." He hesitated, apparently expecting me to go into shock, but I remained calm. A few weeks earlier this would have torn my heart out. But now the peace of the

Lord was within me. My heart had the strength and confidence possible only through Him. The past didn't matter anymore. I knew God was in control now.

Jim continued, "I tried to break the habit many times before, but I just couldn't. I felt hopelessly trapped. Finally, I made up my mind that I was going to kick the habit once and for all and I admitted myself to the hospital. The doctor said that he'd put me on methadone, a replacement drug. I might have to stay on that drug for many years but it would allow me to live a more normal kind of life.

"At first, I refused and said that I didn't want to substitute one drug for another. I wanted to get off drugs completely. He insisted on the methadone, so I had to agree to take it. But after a few days, I stopped. I told the doctor that I refused to take anymore methadone and if he didn't agree I'd walk out of the hospital. This time he agreed, but said I'd never make it.

"Then today I felt that I just had to get out of the hospital, but the doctor wouldn't release me. He said that I wasn't cured yet. Besides, the tests showed that I had a critical case of hepatitis and would have to be treated for it. But I just couldn't stay another day. I had to get out and come back home; so I signed myself out to release the hospital of any responsibility."

By now we knew that the doctor was wrong. Jim was indeed cured. Amazingly, God had cured him completely of his drug habit in a matter of six days! I asked Jim about the withdrawal pains that always accompany "cold turkey." Withdrawals are so painful that every part of your body feels like it's at the threshold of unendurable pain at the same time. Jim said that he had no withdrawals. The Lord, in His mercy, spared him that.

As Jim spoke, I couldn't help but see the signs of suffering still in his eyes. Although God had worked with such speed and power in curing him of the drug habit, he was left with an emptiness that he didn't know how to fill. I knew that Jesus was the only one Who could fill it.

His story finished, we both sat in silence. It was time to approach him about the retreat. "Jim, there's a retreat for young people this coming weekend," I said. "I can't tell you much about it, but it's something like the one that I went on. I believe it will really help you and I'd like you to go."

I was now pretty anxious. As I waited in silence for him to answer, the phone rang. It was Pat, the coordinator of the retreat. I had spoken to her earlier about the possibility of sending Jim along. She called to ask if I knew whether or not he was going. She had to get the correct count because it was only three days away. I told her I was just in the process of getting the answer and asked her to hang on for a minute.

This phone call seemed too timely to be a coincidence. It made the next step natural. I went back to Jim and said, "The coordinator is on the phone and wants to know if you are going on the retreat." Then I asked, "Would you go—as a favor to me?" He thought for a moment. His answer was barely audible. "OK—I'll go." Then after a few moments, he slowly added, in a tone of desperation, "What could I lose?"

Yes, what could he lose. His voice seemed to say much more. "I'm tired. I can't run anymore. I'll do whatever you say." My heart ached at the obvious pain and loneliness evident in his eyes and his voice. I thanked God for the comfort of knowing that Jesus would take care of him. I went back to the phone. "Yes, Pat, Jim will go."

Three days later I drove Jim to Center Valley where a chartered bus was waiting to take the group to the retreat house which was located in the Pocono mountains. Jim boarded the bus and they left.

As I walked back to the car the pain and loneliness evident in Jim's eyes still lurked in my memory. How I wished that I could take that pain from him. But only God could do that. Yes, in fact, Jesus *already* did it when He took all our pain and suffering with Him on Calvary.

"He was pierced through for our transgressions, He was crushed for our iniquities; The chastening for our well-being fell upon Him, And by His scourging we are healed" (Isaiah 53:5).

I drove home full of hope and yet torn at Jim's obvious struggle to keep going in what seemed to him to be a useless venture. My hope was strong because it was a hope in Jesus. Jim's hope was in me and he couldn't be all that sure of it. But then, there was nothing else. The last six years proved all else failed, his friends, the girls, drugs, motorcycles, rock and roll, the Navy.

Oh yes, the Navy. It seemed like ages ago. How I wanted to blame the Navy. That's where he turned onto drugs. But wasn't blaming an organization or people or situations the world's cop-out for avoiding God. How often I did that. But I could do it no longer. Besides, signs of serious trouble were brewing long before the Navy.

There was that heated argument we had about two weeks before he entered the service. I had just learned that he had been driving his motorcycle at more than eighty miles an hour. I was so furious I prohibited him from riding it and put a lock on it to enforce my decree. He promptly broke the lock, took the cycle, and left home. Over the next two weeks, Dottie and I tried to locate him, but without success. Finally, the day before he was scheduled to leave for the Navy, two of our friends, Larry and Dottie, located him in a nearby motel.

I quickly drove to the motel hoping to reconcile our differences before he left. But, it was as though I were talking to a total stranger. I met with a wall of resistance so strong that every effort to persuade him to come home for just this one last night failed.

In a spirit of defeat, I wished him luck and told him that if he ever needed me I would always be ready and willing to help. He remained completely indifferent. I shook his hand, went back out to my car and drove home with a sick feeling in my stomach at the realization that I had been totally rejected by my only son at a most critical period in his life.

A week later, Dottie was jumping with excitement. We had received a letter from Jim. He wrote it while on the train to boot camp at Great Lakes, Illinois. I couldn't wait to read it.

> "Dear Mom and Dad,
> I'm sorry for all the trouble I caused. I didn't realize it until I found out how lonely I am and how I miss everyone back home. I was too thickheaded to give in and now I'm sorry. I know that's a poor excuse but..."

We were thrilled. Reconciliation did come. I was sure that now, at last, everything would turn out fine. And for a while, I thought it had.

Jim went through boot camp with flying colors. He was then transferred to submarine training school at New London, Connecticut, after which he was assigned to a nuclear submarine.

Things continued to go well until shortly after his submarine pulled into the naval base at Bremerton, Washington, for a complete overhaul. They were stationed there for many months. It left Jim with a lot of free time on his hands. His search for things to occupy himself brought him in contact with a gang that turned him onto drugs and a new decline began.

He soon stopped writing and we didn't know what to

make of it until one day when I received a letter from the brig officer in Seattle, Washington. Fear rose within me as I tore open the letter, knowing instinctively that it was bad news. It read,

"Dear Mr. Priolo,

I sincerely regret to inform you that your service-man is confined in the brig at this station..."

The brig? How could it be? There must be a mistake. He was doing so well.

I quickly wrote to the commanding officer for details. His reply was very well written with the intent of lessening the blow, but the hard fact was that Jim was charged with "Willful disobedience of a superior officer," and was in the brig awaiting trial by court martial.

I paced the floor asking, "Why? Why? Why?" Later, after I gathered my thoughts, I called the local recruiting officer, explained my plight, and then added, "Jim was doing so well. What could possibly have happened?" His answer was very blunt. "The problem with kids now-a-days is that they start taking drugs, then begin breaking regulations and end up getting into all kinds of trouble."

I thought, "What's eating him? He's a real nut. Jim wouldn't do a stupid thing like take drugs. That is just out of the question." Drugs were essentially unheard of in the Bethlehem area at that time. My impression was that they were limited to places like New York City, Chicago, and San Francisco. I was not about to believe that Jim could be involved in drugs. How wrong I was.

A few days later, I got a letter from Jim written from the brig. It was a desperate cry for help. He felt as though everything were crashing in on him and he pleaded with me to come out to Seattle to help him. This was a sudden change in character for Jim. He had never asked for help before. He was always too proud. Little did I know about his drug involvement and how it was affecting him—his will—his rationale. Nevertheless, his cry for help was real. There was no issue. I would not let him face the court martial alone.

I flew to Seattle and registered at a motel for the night. The next day I drove a rented car to the Naval Supply Center where I talked with Jim's defense attorney. He arranged for me to see Jim and spend the better part of the day with him.

It was good to see my son. He looked healthy, but obviously disturbed. As we talked he occasionally rambled irrational philosophies, which I couldn't grasp. His mind seemed to be full of torment and running at high speed. It was all so strange—so different from the Jim I knew. It would be some five years before I would piece together the entire story of what was actually gaining control over Jim's will.

The court martial was scheduled for the next day. I was told that I would be permitted to sit in court and testify regarding Jim's character.

I went back to my motel room where I spent the entire evening trying to prepare a suitable statement for the court. My night was very restless. I tossed and turned until finally about 4:00 A.M. I got up, straining for more ideas and jotting down notes.

The trial took place in a small court room. It was my first experience in court and I felt very uneasy in the foreign atmosphere. I sat in the back of the room listening to accusations, witnesses and cross examinations. The trial seemed to be so long and drawn out. It was obviously going badly for Jim. My testimony didn't help at all.

After some three hours, the members of the court reached a verdict of guilty and read the sentence—

"...This court...sentences you
    to forfeit sixty-four dollars for six months;

to be confined at hard labor for six months;
to be discharged from the service with a
bad conduct discharge and
to be reduced to grade of pay E-1."

I sat motionless as the words echoed throughout the room, each word penetrating the very depths of my heart like a piercing sword. I wanted to cry out, "No, it's not true! This is my son that you're sentencing!" But instead I continued to sit motionless, not believing what I heard. It had to be a horrible nightmare. Slowly I got up and left the court room, my mind fighting against the reality of what had happened.

Later I joined Jim in the office of the defense attorney. It was difficult for either of us to talk. "I came some 2500 miles to try to help you," I said, "but I didn't help at all." Jim said, "But I'm glad you came, Dad." He was straining to hold back the tears. So was I.

The next day was Thanksgiving. I told Jim I would stay overnight so that I could spend part of the holiday with him. It was the only thing left that I could do.

On the way back to the motel, I walked through the park that remained from the Seattle World's Fair. I studied the fountains, the Monorail, and the famous Space Needle hoping their attraction would bring some relief. But all the while the details of the trial continued to torment me. My own son sentenced to six months at hard labor sounded so criminal. I thought that kind of thing happened only in books or on T.V. And the thought of his entire future being ruined by the bad conduct discharge was even worse.

I remembered the defense attorney said that it was routine for the entire case to be reviewed in Washington before the decision would become final. Was that a ray of hope? But no. That must be only a formality. Disobedience of a superior officer was very serious business in the eyes of the military. I was well aware of that from my own service training.

As I continued walking, my mind strained to try to reverse the court's decision. Six months at hard labor—bad conduct discharge—six months at hard labor—bad conduct discharge. The words echoed in my ears over and over until finally the strain was too much. I broke down and cried right there on the Seattle sidewalk. No doubt God's release valve saved my sanity.

When I got back to the motel, I called Dottie and broke the news to her. The next day, I visited Jim. The brig was a lonely place to spend Thanksgiving Day, but I was glad I could be there with him.

Late afternoon, I returned to the airport for my flight home. Traffic was light because of the holiday and there were so few people on the plane that I sat alone surrounded by empty seats.

The monotonous hum of the jet engines as we flew in the darkness of night at 39,000 feet seemed to add to my feeling of despair. I thought of how hopeless it all seemed. Each difficulty Jim got into ended up worse than the previous one. There was just no end to it all. And there were still the problems with Dottie and the other children—a life so full of heartaches, so much useless suffering. Where could I find hope? I didn't know. And yet, Jesus was so close and so willing to help, just waiting for me to ask Him—but I didn't—not yet.

Nevertheless, without my knowledge, God was helping. Within two months, the courts reviewed Jim's case and they did indeed change the sentence. His time was reduced. But more important, his discharge was changed to an honorable one. Thus, his future was cleared.

He would be free to come home soon. I felt he now had

a new lease on life. Thank God I didn't know in advance that his new "freedom" would take him ever deeper into the world of drugs where he would experience the torments of the very pits of hell while still here on earth.

But that was all in the past. Jim was entering a new chapter in his life—a chapter of hope in a mystery to be unraveled on a weekend retreat.

I knew that I must continue praying for Jim during the weekend. Sav suggested earlier that I go on a fast. I had never fasted before, but I wanted to do everything I possibly could, and so I fasted for the entire weekend.

The next morning, Saturday, Sav and I went to his church to pray for Jim. We parked in the back lot of the church and had to go in through the side door. As we did, Sav started to laugh.

"What's so funny?" I asked.

He answered, "Remember the day you agreed to go on the retreat with me? You said that you'd go on the condition that I wouldn't try any tricks, like getting you into church through some side-door."

"How about that!" I thought. "Seems like the Lord took care of that, too."

On Sunday afternoon, I drove to Center Valley to pick up Jim. I was early so I went into the chapel to pray and read Scripture. Betty Jane, Sav's wife, had been on the team that supervised the retreat. She returned by car, ahead of the bus load of people, and rushed over to me, bubbling with excitement. "Jim was beautiful, just beautiful," she said. It was the first time that I had ever heard a grown man called beautiful, but it sounded great. I learned later that Betty Jane had watched the performance of a miracle hour by hour as God transformed Jim's whole being. My anxiety to see him grew.

33

Shortly afterward the bus arrived. I saw Jim beaming from ear to ear. He *was* beautiful. We quickly walked toward each other and embraced. He said, "Dad, I love you." It was the first time I ever heard him say that. Tears of joy streamed down my face. The struggle was over. Suddenly the wounds were all healed. I knew that Jim had met Jesus and Jesus was now in his heart.

My mind raced back over the past two weeks. How miraculously God worked, first in my life and now in Jim's. How masterfully He brought Jim step by step to salvation. It would have been impossible for him to go on the retreat while under the bondage of drugs, especially a drug habit that required a shot every hour or two. But God had led Jim to get rid of the habit just in time to make it possible for him to go on the retreat.

Then there was the methadone. Using it as a substitute for heroin would have kept him at home because the methadone treatment still required a daily visit to the hospital for the drug. Patients were not permitted to administer it to themselves. Therefore, even substituting that habit for a heroin habit would still have made the retreat impossible. God in His supernatural wisdom saw all this as He kept Jim from turning to the methadone. Since then I've read reports that methadone is even more difficult to break away from than heroin. Praise God for His infinite wisdom.

There was even more. Time proved that Jim was miraculously and completely cured of the hepatitis since he never had any recurring symptoms.

Chapter 3

AND MY FAMILY

The family was jumping with excitement. "What's happening? First Dad and now Jim! What's going on during those weekends? We want what you've got. Whatever it is we want it. We've just got to go on one of those weekends." Those were the comments we were getting from the rest of the family. They couldn't help but see the changes that took place in Jim and myself. Questions were flying fast and furious. We really didn't know how to answer because everything happened so quickly. The changes were in our hearts, not our minds. Our familiarity with Scripture was essentially zero, so we didn't know how to translate our heart knowledge into words. In addition, we were told not to talk too much about the details of the retreat because it might make it less effective for the future candidates. As a result we said very little.

They pressed on; my wife, my children, even my son-in-law. All of them were singing from the same sheet of music. "We've got to find out what this mystery is all about." No doubt we did appear mysterious, but how could we explain that Jesus had come into our hearts when we were so ignorant of the scriptural support.

My wife tried to solve the mystery herself by snooping. She found my copy of the Good News for Modern Man, a simplified version of the New Testament. I had picked it up when I was on the retreat and kept it in the top dresser drawer. She thought perhaps this book could give her a clue. As she opened it, she thought, "Hmm, this looks something like a Bible." Her knowledge of the Bible was limited to a black-covered, red-leaved book with a layer of dust over it. She began paging through it. "It *is* a Bible," she said. "Well how about that. They're so secretive that they're even camouflaging the Bible."

Over the next few months the mystery cleared up. Between additional weekend retreats and prayer meetings, other members of the family personally learned about Jesus and accepted Him as Lord and Savior. Even my youngest, six-year-old Shelley, joined us with typical child-like faith. The only holdout was Gina, our sixteen-year-old. She put up a real battle. At first, she reacted with calculated opposition, avoiding us like the plague. At the mention of the name of Jesus, she would disappear. Since we were now talking about Jesus almost continuously, she was spending most of the time in her bedroom.

But the Lord was working out His plan for Gina. It started to unravel one Sunday when the entire family gathered at my house. We ate dinner and then reassembled in the living room to talk about Jesus, all of us, that is, except Gina. She dashed up to the safety of her bedroom.

After a bit of discussion about Scripture, Jim began strumming on the guitar and we all started to sing gospel songs. We soon felt the presence of the Lord and were drawn into prayer for Gina's salvation. It was evident from the prayers being voiced that everyone felt a deep love and compassion for Gina. We were sure that God would answer our prayers. But we didn't realize how fast He would do it.

The next day, Gina just popped out of her shell with a burst of love and enthusiasm. She immediately moved into our discussions about Jesus and the Bible and followed with a commitment to the Lord.

We could hardly believe it. Gina didn't go on a weekend retreat nor a prayer meeting. God dealt with her "alone" in answer to our prayers. We were learning that you can't box in the Holy Spirit. He can use any method He choses to bring people to salvation.

Now we were one complete family in the Lord, all jumping with excitement and running with Jesus Christ. Almost overnight the darkest forces of the devil moved out of our house and the Holy Spirit moved in. Thank You, Lord. How beautifully You united us and brought peace to me and my family.

Chapter 4

THE CLIMB

I immediately returned to church. In fact, I was so eager to do so that I started to go several times a week. On my first Sunday back from the retreat I went to a church in Allentown. During the service I could feel the presence of Jesus Christ all around me. Something was different— Praise the Lord!—I had changed.

We prayed the Apostles' Creed. "I believe in God, the Father Almighty, Creator of heaven and earth, and in Jesus Christ, His only Son our Lord...I believe in the Holy Spirit..." Yes, yes, I believe. I really believe now because I know from experience that it's true. The Creed is no longer just a jumble of memorized words.

As the service proceeded, we came to the section on peace, where it is the practice to read from John 14:27, "Lord Jesus Christ, You said to Your apostles, I leave you peace, My peace I give you..." I thought, "I can't believe my ears. He's talking about peace, the same peace I had been praying for daily during the past three and a half months. He's telling us that Jesus is the source of peace and that He freely gives His peace to us." I thought, "I just learned that a few days ago and now I realize that they've been reading that verse in church for years. But somehow, I never really heard it until today."

It wasn't until later, after I studied the Scriptures, that I learned why this was the first time that I really heard that verse of Scripture loud and clear. In Romans 11:8, I read, "God gave them, (referring to the non-believers), a spirit of stupor, eyes to see not and ears to hear not . . ." Thus, for those who haven't accepted Jesus Christ as Lord and Savior, God has a way of keeping them from understanding the Word of God.

However, once we become believers, this changes. In 2 Corinthians 3:16, St. Paul wrote, "But whenever a man turns to the Lord, the veil is taken away." This tells us that as soon as we become believers, through a mystery that only God understands, we begin to really comprehend the Word of God. This is brought out even more emphatically in 1 Thessalonians 2:13, ". . . the word of God . . . performs its work in you who believe." To paraphrase this loosely, the Bible is understandable to only those who believe in Jesus Christ. In fact, it has been said that the Bible is God's love letter to man so that if someone who doesn't believe in Jesus Christ reads it, he is reading someone else's mail and that is why he doesn't understand it.

Putting all this together, I could now see that in John 14:27, Jesus was offering His peace to believers, (His disciples), not to non-believers. In keeping with this, it was only after I became a believer that Jesus offered His peace to me and it was only then that I felt the peace of God, for the first time. But I had to become a believer first.

The service moved on to the "sign of peace." This was a

relatively recent ritual that was initiated while I was away from the church. I learned about its real significance on the retreat, how it breaks down barriers and brings out the love of God between people. At the retreat it was called the "abrazo" which is the Spanish word for a friendly hug or embrace.

I was floating on cloud nine as the message was read, "and now let us offer each other a sign of peace." Without thinking, I quickly leaned over and lightly embraced the woman on my right. As I turned back, my eyes scanned the congregation in front of me. Something was wrong! No one else embraced. The other parishoners were either politely nodding to one another or they were reluctantly shaking hands.

I came down off cloud nine in a split second. "I really messed this one up," I thought. "It's obvious that these people haven't learned about the 'abrazo' yet." I could feel my face get flushed. I tried to avoid looking at the obvious shock on the face of the woman next to me. I couldn't wait for the service to end so that I could get out of church to the safety of my car.

I eventually got over my embarrassment. As I continued my walk in the Lord, my eyes were opened more and more. I was witnessing some of God's unbelievably beautiful activity in the world. And to think that up until a few weeks ago, I thought that God was too distant to be interested in what I was doing.

My family and I soon learned about the baptism in the Holy Spirit as described in the book of Acts. Fortunately, we were never exposed to narrow doctrine opposed to this baptism, therefore, we didn't have to undo false teachings. We asked for the baptism in the Holy Spirit without hesitation. And God rewarded our faith. Some immediately received the manifestation of tongues.

Others received this blessing later. We knew that this outward sign was God's confirmation that we were baptized in the Holy Spirit so we really desired it.

My wife, Dottie, was the only one in the family who had a problem in this area. She was very hesitant about being prayed over for the baptism in the Holy Spirit. She appeared to have some sort of fear. But one of the men, being over-enthusiastic persuaded her to sit in as they prayed over us. Although she finally agreed, she did so with great reluctance.

When hands were laid on Dottie and the prayers began, an unknown force threw her onto the floor and she began to yell, "I can't do it. I can't do it." Then she started to cry hysterically. I felt a little embarrassed at the time, not knowing why she was acting so peculiarly. I knew nothing about evil spirits. Nor did anyone else there. It would be another year before I would understand this attack by the dark powers of the enemy.

A few days later, I received a new kind of blessing. As I sat in my office, there came, as if in a flash of light, the sudden conviction that I knew, without a doubt, that Jesus was really resurrected bodily from the dead. At the time, I was not familiar with the gift of the word of knowledge that St. Paul refers to in 1 Corinthians 12:8, but later, as I looked back, I realized that that was how this message came to me. In any event, I now had the absolute assurance that the resurrection was true. I just knew it. Sure, I had previously accepted this as fact. But hidden down in the depths of my heart there was just a little bit of doubt that the Lord had to clear up. Now it was clear—not a bit of doubt left.

I was so excited that I picked up the phone and called Sav. I said, "Sav, Jesus was really resurrected from the dead. I know it! I just know it!" Sav couldn't understand why I was so excited about it. Of course Jesus was resurrected from the dead. Sav knew it, so what was all the fuss about? I couldn't explain myself, but I hoped that by now Sav was getting used to my excitement over Jesus.

I soon learned how vital this truth is to our walk with the Lord. God's whole plan for salvation would mean nothing if it were not that Jesus Christ was resurrected from the dead. Sure, He died for our sins, but without the resurrection His death would have been in vain. St. Paul states this very clearly in 1 Corinthians 15:17 as he wrote, "If Christ has not been raised, your faith is worthless; you are still in your sins." God knew how much I wanted to grow in faith and He knew that this knowledge was vital to my growth. This is why He made a special point of driving this truth home. And He drove it right down into the marrow of my bones.

My thirst for Scripture had grown ever since the night that I prayed for Jim with Sav and Denny. I read the Bible every chance I could throughout the day. I wanted to be sure that there was always a Bible at my fingertips, so I kept copies in almost every room in the house and in my car and office. Before I met Jesus, we had one Bible carefully hidden where no one could see it. But since my rebirth, I quickly increased our supply until we had at least one copy of almost every popular version of the Bible and numerous copies of our favorites. In addition, I kept scores of Bibles available as handouts. And our Bibles were no longer hidden. They were out in full view.

Right from the start, I had a tremendous desire to grow in faith and as fast as possible. In Romans 10:17, St. Paul wrote that, "Faith comes from hearing and hearing by the word of Christ" (i.e. the Bible). We began to realize that we cannot grow in faith to any great degree unless we accept the entire Bible as the true Word of God, inspired by the Holy Spirit in its entirety (2 Timothy 3:16). Consequently, we did just that, making the Bible our unquestioned guide in our walk with the Lord.

This didn't occur overnight. We had to overcome a lot of false thinking, especially since we grew up during a period when my church discouraged us from reading the Bible on the basis that we didn't have the ability to interpret it correctly. In addition, the world had many arguments against the Bible. "Some of the stories are not logical," they would say. "Some are myths. The writers were of poor educational background." There were an endless number of arguments, all false, resulting from man's attempt to use his worldly intelligence to interpret the Bible.

But God anticipated all this as He wrote through St. Paul, "For the wisdom of this world is foolishness before God" (1 Corinthians 3:19). Also, "I will destroy the wisdom of the wise, And the cleverness of the clever I will set aside" (1 Corinthians 1:19).

As we continued to pray and study Scripture, the Holy Spirit showed us that the world's arguments were all lies propagated by the devil to keep us from growing in faith and from moving closer to God. And more and more, we were trusting in the Holy Spirit to help us interpret the Bible correctly as God promised in John 14:26: "But the Helper, the Holy Spirit, whom the Father will send in My name, He will teach you all things. . ."

Once we accepted the entire Bible as the truly inspired Word of God, we realized we had taken a big step in faith, since that acceptance had to come by faith, not by the world's logic. In fact, Scripture clearly teaches that this is the only way a true Christian can accept the Bible since "whatever is not from faith is sin" (Romans 14:23). With the Bible as our infallible guide, we began to lean on it, continuously using it as a basis for judging everything that we read or heard.

Nevertheless, our approach didn't give us complete protection, especially at first. Scripture warns us that there are many false teachers who will try to lead us away from the truth (Matthew 24:24, 2 Corinthians 11:13). As a result, we found that at times we were deceived by false teachings. But as we came to learn and understand Scripture better, the Holy Spirit gradually corrected us and we were better able to discern the truth.

Our growing faith took us into the area of healings and miracles. God's Word tells us that Jesus is the same yesterday, today and forever (Hebrews 13:8). Since He healed people more than 1900 years ago, it follows that He heals people today, also. In fact, in Mark 16:17-18, Jesus said that believers will be accompanied by a number of miraculous signs, one of which is that "they will lay hands on the sick and they will recover." He promised us the power of the Holy Spirit to perform these signs when we are baptized in the Spirit (Acts 1:8). Soon after my baptism in the Spirit, I had the opportunity to witness God's power in healing my daughter, Gina.

For several years, Gina had a trick knee that would lock at the most unexpected times. When it locked she was unable to straighten it out and would often have to walk with crutches. The knee would remain stiff for varying lengths of time. In one case, it was four days before it finally loosened.

However, the first time that it locked following my baptism in the Spirit, I took authority in the name of Jesus, laid hands on her and prayed for a healing. God was true to His Word and healed her.

Shortly afterward, my daughter, Pam, also experienced the healing power of God. It happened right after a prayer meeting at nearby Brisson Seminary. She accidently fell and twisted her ankle, causing a severe sprain. It was so bad that she couldn't stand on it, nor even attempt to walk. A friend, John, laid hands on her in prayer and her ankle was healed immediately. She got up, tested it, and became so excited that she jumped up and down and then ran around the room proving that it was really healed.

Over a period of time, the Lord healed me of a number of things; a back problem, an ear infection, a swollen hand, headaches, but probably my most dramatic healing occurred one night at a prayer meeting. Some fellow Christians prayed that my left leg would grow. It was a half-inch shorter than my right leg. As they prayed, my left leg felt a warmth flowing through it as it grew the half-inch, matching perfectly with my right leg.

Perhaps by the world's standards these weren't as dramatic as the kind of healings that took place in the Kathryn Kuhlman meetings, but they were still healings performed by God and very dramatic to us. Thank You, Jesus. May You have all the glory.

Then there were also some unusual miracles in the inanimate world that really thrilled me. One day I had a flat tire. I changed it, put on the spare tire and threw the flat one in the trunk. I planned to fix it when I got home. In the meantime, I inflated it. However, I was so busy attending Christian functions that I didn't have the chance to fix it until two days later. By that time, the tire had lost all its air again. I repeated the whole cycle over, inflating the tire, and a few days later it was flat again. I filled it up a third time. This time I prayed, asking the Lord to keep it inflated until I had time to fix it.

Then, oddly enough, I forgot about it for about a week. At the end of the week, I suddenly remembered the flat tire in my trunk. I quickly checked it and found that it still had a full thirty pounds of air in it. I could hardly believe my eyes, so I left it in the trunk for another week to see if it continued to hold air. It did, so I put it on the car and it held air until it wore out!

I just thanked the Lord for going one better than I had asked by actually fixing the flat tire. There was absolutely no doubt that He did it since the tire went flat three times before it finally held air. And that happened only after I prayed about it.

This experience was soon followed by another. Our washing machine developed a water leak that was flooding the floor. The leak was coming out at the bottom of the tub near its center. I tried to repair it, but found that to do so I would have to remove the tub. And, I needed a special tool that I didn't have.

Having reached an impasse, I did the only thing I could. I prayed and asked the Lord to repair the leak. To my surprise, the leak stopped. I could hardly believe it. I was afraid to share this with anyone because I didn't think they would believe me. Finally I couldn't contain myself and shared it with Sav. I can't be sure that he believed it but at least he was polite when I told him. That was some three and a half years ago. The washing machine has been going strong ever since, although it is a bit noisy.

Chapter 5

THE ROAD GETS ROCKY

It didn't take long to find out that the road can get pretty rocky. We were about five months old in the Lord when my son, Jim, went into a tailspin. He had stopped all his Christian activity and pulled back into a shell. This reversal was triggered by a court case that had been pending for about a year, something left over from his pre-Christian days. He was charged with a criminal offense for carrying two knives strapped to the side of his motorcycle. The charge could bring him a $5000 fine and two years in prison. There were several preliminary hearings throughout the past year and now the date for the trail was finally set. It was the imminence of the trial, weighing heavily on him, that caused Jim to go into a deep depression.

I discussed the case with him several times, offering to go to court to support him. He resisted, saying it would be useless to try because on one of his previous visits he was told that he was as good as convicted and sentenced to prison. He had now slipped back into his old ways, so it was useless to try to persuade him to change his mind. In his present depressed state he became withdrawn, refusing to listen to any further discussion of the case. I stopped trying, but continued to pray for him daily.

Then one day I asked God, "What is really happening to Jim, Lord? Why can't he hang in there and rely on You to help him?" In response, the Lord led me to a verse of Scripture. I had always been very careful about indiscriminately claiming that the Lord led me to a certain verse in the Bible. However, there have been a number of times when I was sure that He really did. This was one of those times.

The scripture was Luke 9:38-39. It read: "And a man in the crowd called out to him, 'Teacher, this boy here is my only son, and a demon keeps seizing him, making him scream; and it throws him into convulsions so that he foams at the mouth; it is always hitting him and hardly ever leaves him alone'" (*TLB*).

I thought, "Surely this must be from the Lord because it fits Jim to a tee. He is my only son and it certainly does appear that some mysterious force is taking hold of him, hurting him and causing him to rebel. Is the Lord telling me that an evil spirit is attacking Jim? If so what can I do about it?"

We still hadn't learned anything about evil spirits so I asked some of the men in our prayer group to help me understand this verse of Scripture in light of my son's difficulties. However, this subject wasn't very popular. In fact, there always seemed to be a sudden silence when anyone mentioned evil spirits. No one in the group cared to discuss that area. I felt sure that by giving me this Bible reference, the Lord was telling me that an evil spirit was attacking Jim, but I didn't know what I could do about it.

I didn't realize that it would be some two years before this mystery would be unraveled.

Two days before the trial, five young Christian friends came over to the house to counsel Jim. But, since Jim had withdrawn into a shell of silence, he refused any counselling. He just hibernated in his room.

So, we decided to gather in the family room to pray for him. After a time of prayer, the Lord spoke through me in prophecy saying, "*Everything will work out all right. Jim will come through fine. And when this all comes to pass, you will look back and see that the Lord did a much better job than you could have hoped for.*" Most of us were not too familiar with prophetic messages at the time. In fact, we weren't even sure this was a prophecy from God until we saw it "come to pass."

The Lord was not through speaking yet. That night while I was asleep, I was suddenly awakened with a message from the Lord. The substance of the message was, "*You must go to court with Jim to support him in his defense. If you don't go you will find yourself wallowing in your sorrow afterwards because without your support his penalty will be severe.*"

This command came as quite a surprise because I hadn't even given any thought recently to the question of accompanying Jim. I had put that question to rest a week or two back when Jim made it so plain that he didn't want my help.

Nevertheless, I now had a command from the Lord. It was the first time that the Lord specifically directed me to do something. However, it came through so strong and clear that I had no doubt that it was from Him. I knew that I must go to court regardless of what Jim thought.

Jim was working nights at the time and when he came home the next morning, I explained to him that the Lord had directed me to go to court with him. Realizing that in his present backslidden state he would refuse my company, and probably challenge the truth about the Lord speaking to me, I added firmly, "Whether you agree or not I must go. I'll either drive down with you or I'll drive down without you. Either way I will go. I will not disobey the Lord."

The trial was scheduled for the next day at a courthouse located in the state of New Jersey. We drove down together. I prayed almost continuously from the moment I got out of bed. We arrived early and were immediately escorted into the District Attorney's office, where two men questioned Jim. They asked about a lawyer. Jim said he didn't have any because he couldn't afford one. They reprimanded him for not notifying them early enough to have the court appoint a lawyer for Jim. It was too late now for them to do so.

The two men then went over the case with us. They read the charge and suggested that Jim plead guilty, adding that they would ask the court's mercy in settling the case. They explained that this would avoid the cost of a trial by jury and possibly imprisonment. Hopefully, the case would be settled with only a fine, although there was no guarantee against imprisonment.

Some of this didn't sound all that bad. But the frightening part of the proposal was the thought of Jim ending up with a criminal record. It really worried me, but I tried to appear calm on the outside. I said, "The fine doesn't bother me, but doesn't this mean that Jim would have a permanent criminal record?" They agreed and quickly went into a huddle for a few minutes, after which they made an alternate proposal. "We could re-write the entire charge," they said, "and throw it into a miscellaneous category, a catchall. This would take it out of the criminal category and make it a misdemeanor, something similar to disturbing the peace. But you still would have to pay the fine."

I could hardly believe my ears. Their alternate proposal sounded too good to be true. It would completely wipe out the possibility of a jail sentence and Jim's record would remain clean. I knew that the Lord had kept His Word and interceded. I leaned over to Jim and whispered, "This looks like the work of the Lord. I suggest that we accept it." He quickly agreed.

We were told to wait in the courtroom until Jim's case came up. The judge would have to approve the plea. There was no guarantee that he would. We sat in the courtroom for the balance of the day. As I listened to the other cases being tried, it became apparent that the judge was very uncompromising with the defendants. My concern grew so I said, "This judge is really tough, Jim. Who is he? Did you ever see him on any of your previous visits here?" He answered, "Yes, he's the one who got so mad at me that he told me I was as good as convicted and sentenced to prison."

I was sorry I asked. Now I really started to worry. The fact that Jim didn't have a lawyer wasn't helping.

Jim was called at about 4:00 P.M. His was the last case of the day. I prayed, "Lord, please use my presence to help Jim." When Jim took the stand I was surprised to see an immediate change come over the judge. Instead of the formidable man I had listened to all day, he became unusually pleasant.

He questioned both Jim and me. Each time he questioned Jim, I held my breath as I prayed that he'd give the right answer. I hadn't appreciated the agony that Jim had been going through. A year of waiting for the case to come to trial was a heavy burden to carry.

At one point he asked, "Why did you plead guilty?" Jim was obviously tired. He tried to be completely honest as he answered, "Because I wanted to get the case over with." I thought, "Oh no, now he did it."

But the judge didn't flinch. The case continued. Finally the judge was finished with the interrogation and said to Jim, "Do you have anything you wish to say?"

"Yes," Jim replied.

I could see the judge lean forward as if to be sure not to miss a word. I held my breath again, "Please, Jim, don't blow the whole thing." I was afraid to listen.

Quietly Jim answered, "I just want to say that I didn't know that it was against the law to have knives in your possession."

The judge slid back in his chair, heaved a sigh and said with a smile, "Well, now you know."

He accepted the plea and promptly dismissed the case. Then we all but flew out of the courtroom and quickly went to the prosecutor's office to pay the fine. As Jim picked up the receipt, the prosecuting attorney walked up to Jim with a puzzled look on his face and said, "You sure got a good deal. In fact, even with a lawyer the deal couldn't have been better!" We smiled. If he only knew that we did have a lawyer. Jesus was our Lawyer and He did a far better job than any human lawyer could have done.

Yes, the prophecy that the Lord gave me was rapidly showing fulfillment—"When it all comes to pass you will look back and see that the Lord did a much better job than you could have hoped for." We looked back and knew that God wanted us to sit through all those cases to see how really stern the judge normally was but that Jesus could still soften his heart.

This miraculous performance stirred Jim's heart again. He came out of his depression and the next day recommitted his life to Jesus, pouring himself back into prayer and the Bible.

Soon Jim fell in love with Kathy, a beautiful, Spirit-filled Christian. At the time, Kathy had made preliminary arrangements to enter a religious order and become a nun. However, the Lord interceded and it wasn't long before Jim and Kathy decided to get married.

Plans were made to have the wedding in our church. About two hundred fifty people were invited, half of them charismatic. We were all excited during the weeks of preparation. The service was specially prepared for a charismatic wedding including both the singing of Christian songs by the congregation and singing in the Spirit.

Finally, the day of the wedding came. Two young girls sang the entrance hymn as Kathy walked down the aisle. I felt God's presence all around us. The ceremony continued for an hour and a half intermixed with song and worship as wave after wave of God's power fell over us. Tears of joy could be seen throughout the church. It was as though God had brought us all to a beautiful peak of worship.

During the singing, my sister, Pat, and her daughter, Mary Lou, were so overwhelmed by the power of God that they spontaneously gave their hearts to Jesus.

And so it was that the Lord continued to do a "much better job" than we could have hoped for.

Chapter 6

A HEAVENLY LANGUAGE

St. Paul wrote that it was his wish that all believers would speak in tongues (1 Corinthians 14:5). Tongues, the heavenly prayer language that many believers have received from God since the first day of Pentecost (Acts 2:4). From the moment that I learned about tongues, I had a tremendous desire to have this blessing that comes as part of the package with the baptism in the Holy Spirit.

It was the practice in our prayer group that each person would go through a series of teachings on the baptism in the Holy Spirit before being prayed over to receive it. Therefore, a few weeks after my rebirth, I began attending the teachings, looking forward to the time when I would receive the baptism.

It seemed like a long wait, but the day finally came when I was about two months old in the Lord. There were six or eight of us that were prayed over simultaneously. Most of the others received tongues, but I did not. I was disappointed, but hopeful that the gift of tongues would ultimately come.

Weeks went by and then months, but still without success. I could not understand it. Why did so many of my friends receive tongues so easily while I was having so much difficulty? There were several times when I felt a kind of strange language churning around in my mind, but I wasn't sure and felt that I would appear too foolish if I tried to speak the words out loud. I waited, expecting that if this were really tongues, some overpowering force would move the words out of my mouth. But it never happened.

In the meantime, I studied and re-studied Scripture relating to tongues to try to find out why I was not successful in receiving it. I read in 1 Corinthians 14:1, "... desire earnestly the spiritual gifts..." I thought, "But I do desire tongues and it's a spiritual gift. In fact, this is the greatest desire that I have right now."

Then I read in Mark 16:17 where Jesus said, "And these signs will accompany those who have believed: in My name they will cast out demons, they will speak with new tongues." I thought, "I am a believer, so according to the Scriptures, I should absolutely be able to speak in new tongues."

As time went by, I occasionally discussed this subject with my friends. There were some strong feelings about the significance of tongues. Some felt that unless you spoke in tongues you were not baptized in the Spirit. Others felt that to speak in tongues was not necessarily required proof of the baptism.

I wasn't sure. Nevertheless, I still felt that it would be a real comfort to be blessed with tongues and thus remove any doubt.

Five months had passed since I prayed for the baptism and I still hadn't received tongues. Finally, one day while I was driving home from work, my desire became so great that I began pleading with the Lord: "Why haven't I received tongues, Lord? What must I do to receive? There are so many reasons why I need a new language. It would be so useful for my edification. It would help me minister to people for healing and other needs. I must have it before I could pray sincerely for others to receive tongues." My pleading went on and on. I wasn't sure at the time that the Lord took all this into account. I thought I'd remind Him anyway.

As I continued to drive homeward, my desire grew to such intensity that I started to deliberately imitate tongues by making up words that sounded like gibberish. I yelled the words out as rapidly and as loudly as I could. After a minute or so, the words suddenly changed to an orderly language. I could hardly believe my ears. "That's not gibberish anymore," I thought. "Those are real words coming out of my mouth. I don't understand them, but I'm not making them up anymore."

The words were beautiful. They sounded oriental. As I continued praying in tongues, thoughts raced through my mind about how I had received my language. Yelling out words in gibberish was really an act of faith. All along I was waiting to get my language with very little effort of my own. Now that I opened my mouth and started talking, I gave the Holy Spirit something to work with. I was so happy and excited that I drove right past my house. I kept driving around the block just so that I wouldn't have to stop praying in this beautiful language.

I felt as though I had taken a giant step in my relationship with the Lord and moved into a higher level of worship. It didn't matter anymore who was right in the argument about whether or not tongues was proof of the baptism in the Spirit. In any case, there was now no doubt I was baptized in the Spirit.

I couldn't get over the fact that the Holy Spirit was manifesting Himself through me by giving me the words that were coming out of my mouth. It was just too much for me to think about.

That evening, I called my daughter, Pam, who was living alone in an apartment at the time. She also was having difficulty with the heavenly language. When she was prayed over for the baptism she did receive a few words. However, her vocabulary had not increased significantly. That was five months before. I said, "Pam, I think that I know what's holding you back." After explaining how I had received tongues, I said, "Next time you come over I'll pray for you and show you what to do to increase your vocabulary." She became so excited that she said, "I'm not waiting another minute. I'll be right over."

When Pam arrived we went into one of the bedrooms for privacy and I explained, "You have to yell out all kinds of made up words. You'll feel very foolish but you must be willing to allow yourself to feel foolish. This is your part of stepping out in faith." Then I laid hands on her and prayed in my own tongue.

Pam started to speak out in gibberish just as I did. In about two minutes the words changed to an orderly language. I could see the excitement in her face as she recognized the new language that was flowing from her mouth. She continued to pray in tongues for a while, then burst out laughing and praising the Lord.

In view of her immediate success, we knew that both Pam and I had had the same problem. We really didn't know how to cooperate with the Holy Spirit. The secret was that we had to start using our voice with boldness, so that the Holy Spirit could take over. *We* had to begin speaking before the Spirit gave the utterance.

Now that I really experienced praying in tongues, I thought back and clearly remembered two previous occasions when words in a strange language were churning in my mind. I know now that both times the Lord was trying to give me tongues, but my lack of boldness, that is my fear of speaking out in the presence of other people, kept me from receiving the language. However, once the Lord brought me to a place where I could speak out uninhibited (alone in my car), the heavenly language came out of my mouth. In view of my experience and Pam's, whenever I pray for people who have difficulty receiving tongues, I encourage them to step out in boldness in the way Pam and I did and success usually follows.

One evening I got a call to help minister to a friend, John, who was sick. I called my son, Jim, and asked if he would join me and he agreed. When we arrived at John's house, several other Christians were there. We proceeded to pray for John and since most of us were baptized in the Spirit, we prayed in the Spirit (in tongues).

John's wife, Marge, however, did not pray in tongues. I didn't notice this myself, but in the course of the evening the subject of tongues came up and Marge said, "I believe I've been baptized in the Spirit but I haven't received tongues. I really want my language, but the Lord hasn't seen fit to give it to me yet. I'm open to receiving tongues and when the right time comes, I'm sure He'll give them to me."

Jim and I glanced at each other and I knew we were both thinking the same thing. Quickly, I asked, "Marge, do you sincerely want to speak in tongues?"

"Yes, I really do," she answered.

"Then you'll receive your language tonight. Let's go into the kitchen. It's a bit more convenient there."

We left the living room and went into the kitchen for privacy and I began to teach Marge about receiving tongues. I assured her, "Marge, if you really want tongues you will receive them now. When you received the

61

baptism in the Holy Spirit, all the gifts of the Spirit were included in the package. However, you have to be open and willing in receiving them. St. Paul tells us to 'desire earnestly spiritual gifts'" (1 Corinthians 14:1). "Now let me explain how you can help yourself receive tongues."

Then I explained how Pam and I had received them and told her she had to step out in faith and use her voice. As I spoke I could see Marge getting excited. She kept saying, "Yes. Yes." Finally I said, "OK, we're going to lay hands on you and pray in tongues. When we do, start using your voice."

But before I could pray, she suddenly started to speak out in a beautiful heavenly language. My first reaction was, "No, wait. We didn't even start to pray yet. You're not following my system." Then we all burst out laughing. Who needs a system? Marge had finally stepped out in faith and the Holy Spirit took over. Praise the Lord!

My excitement over praying in the Spirit never subsided to any significant degree. From the moment I received tongues, I had an insatiable thirst to pray in this language every chance I could. I prayed in my new language in the morning, in the evening, while walking or jogging or driving. The words quickly became clearer and smoother and the Lord changed the language completely several times as though to give me new excitement with each new language.

I was thankful in so many ways for this heavenly language. It was easier to pray by alternating between English and tongues. Often, when I had difficulty praying in English, I overcame it by first praying in the Spirit for a while and then going into English.

According to Acts 2:4 I was able to pray in tongues only because through a deep mystery of God the Holy Spirit was giving me the words to say.

It didn't matter that I didn't understand the words.

One writer expressed my feelings very well when he wrote, "When I pray in tongues, I don't know what I'm saying, but I know what I'm doing. I'm letting the Holy Spirit pray through me to God." Thus, I knew this was a perfect way of praying since the Holy Spirit knew much better than I what to pray about. In fact, I would learn this one day in a very dramatic way.

The time came a year after I first received the manifestation of tongues. It was a Friday in November. I had the day off from work. I got up at 6:00 A.M. and went into the family room to pray and worship the Lord. This had now become my habit. As I prayed in the Spirit, I began to experience unusual difficulty in getting the words out of my mouth. After praying a few words, I would run out of breath and have to stop to recuperate. I would pray a few more words and run out of breath again. This continued for the entire prayer period. It was much like running out of breath while jogging, except that I wasn't jogging.

I wondered if I might be undergoing some sort of satanic attack. When Dottie and Gina woke up I asked them to pray with me in the hopes that this would drive off the attack. The difficulty continued. Finally, I thought of the verse in Romans 8:26 where Paul wrote that sometimes we don't know exactly how to pray so the Holy Spirit prays through us with such deep feeling that it cannot be expressed in words. This is referred to by some as praying in travail.

Yes, that was the answer. I never really understood what praying in travail meant before because I had never experienced it until now. And I was learning that there's nothing like personal experience to drive a piece of Scripture home. I was now praying in travail just as Paul explains it. This was a prayer of intercession for someone, but I did not know who that someone was or what his need was. This was why the Holy Spirit took over. The whole process was another one of God's deep mysteries, too deep for my limited mind to grasp. But I accepted it all by faith based on God's Word in Romans 8:26.

Now that I knew I was praying in travail, I felt better about doing it. It was not a satanic attack. Instead someone was in need of help and God had chosen me to pray for that person. This very thought gave me motivation to keep praying as much as I could.

During mid-afternoon an unusual thing happened. While praying in the Spirit, the word "Marietta" came out of my mouth interwoven with the words of the heavenly language. I thought, "Marietta, the Italian name that my parents used in addressing my sister, Mary. How strange that her name should happen to come out of my mouth mixed in with the heavenly language." Mary was now in Phoenix. I promptly dismissed the thought, assuming it had no significance, and continued praying in travail on and off until I went to bed that night.

The next morning I got up early and went into the family room to pray again. But now the prayer burden was completely gone. In it's place was a tremendous feeling of exuberance. I felt so happy I started to praise the Lord and sing at the top of my voice.

Then toward mid-morning the doorbell rang. I answered it. Standing in front of me, beaming all over, was my sister Mary. I couldn't believe my eyes. Mary should be in Phoenix. She started talking but I wasn't listening. I must have gone into momentary shock as the truth hit me. After I recovered, Mary tried to explain how she happened to be at my house. As she did the remaining pieces of the puzzle started to fall into place.

Five years earlier, when she flew to Phoenix, she developed trouble in one of her ears. This resulted in the loss of hearing in that ear. She had good reason to believe that the flight in the plane was the nucleating cause. She never wanted to fly again for fear of losing the hearing in the other ear. Consequently, she hadn't been home since.

But yesterday morning, Friday, at the breakfast table, she talked about the fact that many of us, including my father, who lives with me, and most of my brothers and sisters would be meeting together in Bethlehem, Pennsylvania. The reason for the reunion was that we would all be attending a family wedding on Saturday. Mary thought how nice it would be to join us, but knew she couldn't because of her fear of flying. Then suddenly, unknown to Mary, God moved in and all her fears disappeared. Without further hesitation she went ahead with the arrangements to fly home.

The flight was a complete success. There was no ear trouble and she felt peaceful during the entire trip.

We were all blessed by Mary's presence and spent many hours together, my father and most of his children, talking over old times and updating one another.

There was no doubt in my mind that my prayer burden was indeed for Mary. The Lord used me to pray for her need. It wasn't a matter of life or death, but God is interested in giving us joy. In John 16:24, Jesus said, "...ask and you will receive that your joy may be full." Not only did God bring joy to Mary, but He brought joy to us all as we spent precious hours together.

And how thoughtful of the Lord to confirm this conclusion by giving me Mary's unique identification, "Marietta," not Mary or some other version of Mary, but precisely the pet name that could only refer to my sister. It was clear that the Lord wanted me to be absolutely sure by leaving an unmistakable sign. Thank You, Jesus!

As the excitement of this experience wore off, I was to have a second opportunity for intercessory prayer. However, this time it was a matter of life or death, not just for pleasure. It occurred a few months after my first experience. I was driving to work one morning, praying in the Spirit, when suddenly I had great difficulty in getting the words out of my mouth. But now I knew at once that I had a burden to pray for someone. Again I didn't know why or for whom. Nevertheless, I felt driven to pray and continued to do so right up until I was ready to enter the door of the plant. Then the burden left me. I thought, "Someday I'll learn why I prayed." Then I put the experience out of my mind as I became involved in my work.

A half-hour later, my daughter, Pam, called full of excitement. She said, "Dad, have I got something to tell you! This morning as I was getting dressed I heard an automobile screech to a stop outside my apartment. I knew there must have been an accident so I started to pray in the Spirit. As soon as I got dressed, I ran outside still praying in tongues. There, lying in the street, was a six-year-old boy surrounded by people. He had been hit by a car and thrown about fifteen feet. When I arrived on the scene, he got up and didn't seem to have anything wrong with him."

I quickly asked when this happened. Pam's answer proved that the time coincided with the period when I had the prayer burden on the way to work. Now, I was the excited one. I explained to Pam how the Lord seemed to have led me to support her in prayer for this boy.

That evening it was reported that the boy had been taken to the hospital for examination, found to have no injuries, and immediately discharged. There was no question in our hearts that our combined intercessory prayers resulted in God's protection of this child. Thank You, Lord. May all the glory be Yours.

I was now more thankful than ever that I had received tongues. How exciting it was to be used by the Lord through this gift to intercede for people in time of need. I wondered, "The Lord revealed who I prayed for and why in these two cases, but is it possible that there were other times when I prayed in the Spirit for people's needs and did not know it?" It was enough to make my head swim.

Chapter 7

REACH OUT

I came from a large family. There were nine of us. My brothers and sisters were all "good Christians," attending church regularly. Nevertheless, the only ones I was sure were saved were my sister, Pat, and her daughter, Mary Lou. To my knowledge, none of the others openly said they accepted Jesus Christ as their Lord and Savior, so I concluded that they were not saved. Right or wrong, that was my conclusion and my burden for them was heavy because I wanted them all to have eternal life. I gave much thought to this problem, trying to determine what I could do about it.

Shortly after I was saved, I wanted to rush off and talk to my brothers and sisters about Jesus. But I held back because I wasn't sure how to go about it. As time went by, I began to feel frustrated about my inability to come up with a plan. My feelings of frustration grew worse as I saw many other new Christians who did rush off to try to lead their loved ones to salvation only to experience disaster.

I learned, though much later, that the problem was that many new Christians had not grown in the fruit of love yet. As a result, they came on so strong that they ended up driving their loved ones further away from the Lord. I hoped that I could avoid that mistake.

It was now some ten months since I committed my life to Jesus. I had difficulty holding back any longer. Many of my brothers and sisters were scattered across the country. I decided that the best way to reach them all would be with a written testimony. Hopefully, when they would read how miraculously Jesus had been working in our lives, they would jump at the opportunity to ask Jesus to come into their hearts.

Over the next few weeks, I prepared an eleven-page testimony. Before mailing the letters out, I gathered my family to pray over them. I thought, "If only one brother or sister were led to salvation as a result of the letters, it would be well worth the effort I put into them." I mailed the letters and waited. Within ten days two replies came back. The theme in both was the same. "Lou, I'm glad that you finally found Jesus... but please don't preach religion to me... you see, I've known Jesus all my life."

This upset me. They missed the message completely. OK, so they knew Jesus all their lives, but I wasn't talking only about knowing Jesus. Even Satan knows Jesus, to use the term loosely. When He walked on the earth demons often called Jesus the Son of God. I was talking about accepting Jesus as Lord and Savior, having a personal relationship with Him, conversing with Him, committing your life to Him and serving Him.

That comment about preaching religion seemed to come with an extra barb. I didn't think I was preaching religion. My letter was about a Person, a Person who was crucified, a Person who died for our sins and was resurrected so that we might have eternal life. This wasn't some kind of religion. This basic truth about Jesus is the heart of all man's desire and ability to have a personal relationship with God.

Another week passed. My sister, Pat, called and told me that the Holy Spirit was stirring up something with my brother, Tom. This came as a surprise to me because if I were to guess, he would be the last one I'd expect to show an interest in my letter. The reason is that he was the only one in the family with whom I wasn't on speaking terms. The last time that I saw him we had gotten into an argument that became so heated that we hadn't talked to each other since. That was five years ago. How strange that the first signs of life should come from Tom.

A Penn State graduate in Civil Engineering, Tom was now working for the government in Washington, D.C. He was always a self-confident and strong-willed person. As a result, his first reaction to my letter was really one of brutal rejection.

He, too, sat down and started to write me a letter much like that of my sisters. "I've always known Jesus," he wrote. "It's about time that you finally got to know Him..." I was becoming pretty familiar with that tune. But Tom never finished the letter. He was diverted by a crisis within his own family. By now, I knew that there was nothing more effective than a crisis to draw one's attention to God.

The crisis was with Tom's oldest daughter, Anita. After eleven years of marriage and three children, she was planning to divorce her husband, Bill. Divorce in our family was unheard of, so Anita's divorce announcement came as a tremendous shock to Tom.

But he was not about to give up without a fight. Now that he saw the imminence of this threat, Tom decided to set the entire family straight on the subject. He called all nine of his children together to discuss divorce. In summary, he decreed, "There's no one in my family who will ever get a divorce!" But his decrees no longer seemed to carry the authority they did in the past since most of his children were now pretty well grown. He must have sensed this and realized that he was grasping at straws. How opportune that my letter should arrive just as this pending tragedy was coming to a head.

In the meantime, my letter was passing through the hands of each member of Tom's family. They started to see it as a possible answer for Bill and Anita. Although Tom was still sure that the letter had no message for him, he did hope that it might have something for Bill and Anita and passed it on to them. The pressure was now on for them to go to one of "those prayer meetings" to see what it was all about. It might straighten out their marriage.

Bill and Anita couldn't have cared less about saving a dead marriage. They argued bitterly over the advice to go to *any* meeting. However, they felt that they were under tremendous pressure to comply. As a result, one evening, in the heat of an argument, they declared a truce long enough to go to a prayer meeting. And then things started to happen.

The meeting, held in the Baltimore area, was made up of Spirit-filled Christians of all denominations. Singing, praying, and the gifts of the Spirit were manifested during the evening. Bill and Anita looked on in complete bewilderment since this type of worship looked so strange to them. But they stayed, though reluctantly, to see this "thing" through.

Toward the end of the evening, Bill heard someone call out to him, "*Bill*." Not realizing that it was the Lord, he turned to the person next to him and said, "What?" The man answered, "I didn't say anything."

Then the group started to sing the Lord's prayer.

Suddenly, Bill saw a vision. As he later wrote to me in a letter, "All the lights seemed to go out except for a bright beam of light in the center of the group. And there stood Jesus in silhouette form with His arms outstretched saying, '*Bill, why did you wait so long?*'" Bill continued, "His eyes were so full of compassion, love and forgiveness that I spoke to Him by opening up my heart and He came in."

Over the next few weeks things moved into high gear. Bill's conversion was so dramatic that it was quickly followed by Anita's. Anita had more than a marital problem. For years she had had a tipped uterus. The ailment was getting progressively worse. The pain was now so severe that the doctor scheduled her for an operation. However, in the meantime, Bill felt led to pray that Jesus would heal her and as he did Anita felt the uterus move right into place. She was healed. Praise the Lord! As Bill and Anita related these things and many others to my brother Tom, he concluded that they must surely be exaggerating. But as new accounts kept coming in almost daily, Tom's walls of disbelief began to crumble.

During this period, Tom continued to try to write me a letter of rejection. He started it under three separate occasions. However, he just could not complete it and each time felt compelled to destroy what he had written.

Tom's wife, Edna, was a bit more open, and under her influence they both attended some prayer meetings to "see for themselves." Within a few weeks they both conceded to the Lord and committed their lives to Jesus. A short time later, Tom's entire family had committed their lives to Jesus and were baptized in the Spirit.

We just praised the Lord for bringing two complete families to salvation. It was clear that God is interested in saving *entire families.* Between Tom's family and mine, plus my sister, Pat, and her daughter, there were now seventeen new reborn Christians in the Body of Christ, all within about a year. Thank You, Lord Jesus, for being our Savior.

A few months later I arranged to visit Tom, who lives in Chevy Chase, Maryland, just outside Washington, D.C. I went alone on this first visit. I took advantage of the freedom of driving alone and planned to pray and sing in the Spirit as I drove down. I was having a merry time and soon felt as though I was being escorted by angels. But about halfway down, after some two hours of praying and singing, I ran out of steam. My voice started to give out so I drove the rest of the way in silence.

When I arrived at Tom's it was still relatively early in the morning and it looked as though no one was up. I hesitated a moment and wondered just how it would be to see Tom for the first time after five years of silence. Then I walked up and knocked on the door. It swung open and Tom immediately greeted me with open arms. We embraced right there in the doorway and I knew that the past was finally forgiven. I thanked the Lord for this miraculous reunion that only He could perform.

The rest of the family woke up and we quickly began to fill each other in on what was happening. We were so excited that we didn't stop for a minute. This reunion was like none I had ever experienced with Tom and his family before. It was just too much to be in the middle of all this excitement Jesus brought to us.

Later in the day, Bill and Anita came over to Tom's house and joined in the discussions. They were so excited in what the Lord was doing that there was no holding them back either. As the day progressed, I noticed that any time that Bill or Anita had a problem or question they would stop for a moment and talk to the Lord and soon they would have the answer. I thought, "They must have a direct line to Jesus. I never saw anything like it." It really puzzled me, especially since they were only a few months old in the Lord.

Some weeks back Tom had started holding prayer meetings at his house and had one scheduled for this night. He had always invited his entire family. Usually most of them attended. However, Tom's daughter, Lorraine, was having no success in bringing her husband, Paul. Paul was still in the fearful stage. Because of this fear, he refused to attend the prayer meetings. Tom, nevertheless, called Paul and said, "Paul, my brother, Lou, is visiting and will be at the prayer meeting tonight. I'd like you to come with Lorraine." Paul said, "OK, I'll be there."

It wasn't until he hung up the phone that Paul fully realized that he was going to attend a *prayer* meeting, something he had previously decided he would never do. He was so furious that he could've kicked himself around the block. As much as he wanted to renege on his agreement he couldn't bring himself to call Tom back. He decided to attend and sweat it out.

That night during the prayer meeting, I felt led to prophesy. As I uttered the words that the Lord was giving me, Paul heard a loud rumble of thunder that startled him. He quickly looked around the room to see how the others were reacting to the thunder. But he saw no reaction, just the quiet attention to the words of prophecy.

Then he heard another burst of thunder and at the same time his chest felt like it was on fire. Since no one else stirred, Paul started to suspect that God had something to do with what was happening.

After the meeting, Paul asked Lorraine if she had heard any thunder. She didn't nor did anyone else. When they mentioned it to me, I remembered that I had read something about thunder in the book of Revelation. I then read in Revelation 6:1, "I saw when the Lamb broke one of the seven seals, and I heard one of the four living creatures saying as with a voice of thunder, 'Come.'" And there was another reference in verse 14:2, "And I heard a voice from heaven . . . like the sound of loud thunder . . ."

Paul was becoming more and more convinced that the thunder and the tremendous warmth in his chest were signs of God trying to reach out to him. It was only a matter of a few more days and then Paul also committed his life to Jesus.

When I came back home, I talked with the family about Bill and Anita seeming to have a direct line with the Lord. It was really puzzling. How could they get answers from the Lord so easily when I had been trying for well over a year and seemed to be completely unsuccessful.

I asked the Lord why I couldn't get answers from Him the way Bill and Anita did. It was as though I had asked a loaded question because the Lord started to reveal to me the many times when He did speak to me very clearly.

There was the time right after my first retreat when I was full of anxiety because Jim left home and the Lord gave me the assurance that things were in control as He told me, "When you ask me to do something don't tell me how to do it."

Then there was the time the Lord woke me up in the middle of the night and told me to go to court with Jim to help in his defense. I accepted it without a doubt at that time. Did I forget it now?

Then the Lord seemed to say, "Who gave you that urging that took you out into the shop the day Sav talked to you about the retreat? And how did you get that revelation about the resurrection? And who urged you to pray in travail for Mary and that boy who was hit by a car?"

I began to get the picture that the Lord had been

talking to me quite a bit. I was looking for Him to talk to me the same way He was talking to Bill and Anita and overlooking the fact that He was already talking to me in other ways, through a soft inner voice, urgings, impressions, through Scripture and through other people.

I also suspected that I probably was being overcautious in accepting messages from the Lord, that is, He was talking to me more often than I realized.

Later, Bill and Anita found they were having the opposite problem. They apparently were not cautious enough and found that some of the messages they thought came from God did in fact come from the enemy. As a result, at times they were deceived. It was apparent that we were all learning, but in different ways.

Chapter 8

A MIXED-UP CAR

"For we are not fighting against people made of flesh and blood but against persons without bodies—the evil rulers of the unseen world, those mighty satanic beings and great evil princes of darkness who rule this world; and against huge numbers of wicked spirits in the spirit world. So use every piece of God's armor to resist the enemy whenever he attacks..." (Ephesians 6:12-13, *TLB*)

A battle with the unseen world? Wicked spirits without bodies? Spirits who rule this world? What about the human beings that we have always thought of as the rulers? It would be quite a while before I would begin to understand this piece of Scripture.

Paul was writing to the believers not the unbelievers, telling them to wear their (spiritual) armor as protection in the battle that is continually taking place with the evil spirits who are in effect the real rulers of this world, the rulers behind the scenes.

This was not the way I had it put together when I

accepted Jesus as my Lord and Savior. He came into my life in such a dynamic way that I thought He wiped out all the dark mysterious things that were plaguing me. It wasn't long before I started to learn first hand that the devil does indeed continue to work hard at attacking Christians, in fact, perhaps more so than non-Christians. My awakening started with a car that seemed to be under the rule of the dark powers of this world.

In January, just prior to my rebirth, Frank, my son-in-law, bought a car from a neighbor. It appeared to be in very good shape mechanically. In fact, it didn't even have a scratch on it. However, right after the verbal agreement was made by Frank to buy it, the owner had an accident and damaged the right side of the car, though not too seriously.

Two weeks later, we were having the winter's worst blizzard. The snow was coming down so fast and the winds were so strong that the snowplows were unable to stay ahead of the snowdrifts. I was thankful that I was enjoying the warmth and comfort of home when in walked Frank. One look at him and I knew there was trouble in the air. He explained apologetically that the visibility was so bad that he ran into a snowbank. So he hitchhiked a ride some two miles to my house for help.

I got dressed in warm clothing, picked up a couple of shovels and we drove out to the site to dig out the car. The front end had really run deep into the snowbank and the entire car was hung up in the snow so that the wheels could not get any traction. After shoveling for about an hour, we got the snow clear from the rear wheels, only to find that both rear tires were flat. How they both could go flat at the same time was difficult for me to comprehend.

We drove back home, picked up two spare tires that were already mounted on wheels and replaced the flat tires. The car was so deep in the snow that it took several more hours of shoveling under the cold, driving winds before we finally brought it into the clear.

Some months later, my daughter, Gail, (Frank's wife) had an accident causing damage to the left side of the car pretty well matching the damage on the right side. Soon afterward, Frank had an accident smashing the front fender and bumper. Before he even had time to consider what to do about the damages, he began having a serious problem with the starter. The difficulty continued until finally the engine wouldn't start at all.

I volunteered to help, but we didn't have much success. In fact, things got worse. The battery went dead and the starter failed. We overhauled the starter and borrowed a battery but still had no success in starting the engine.

Finally, we decided to tow the car from Frank's apartment to my house where we could work in the shelter of my garage. We checked the compression and found it to be down to fifty pounds in each cylinder. It should have been closer to one hundred and forty pounds. We also found that the timing belt was in bad shape and had to be replaced. We decided we might as well give the engine an overhaul.

We put in new rings, ground the valves and replaced the timing belt along with some lesser jobs. But during every step of the way, we seemed to be plagued with mysterious problems. At first, we tried to laugh them off. Everyone has problems with cars. We started to blame them on "Murphy's Law," a subtle reference often made in jest by engineers to lighten the seriousness of difficult problems. The law is said to read, "If anything *can* go wrong, it *will* go wrong." The law sure described what was happening to us.

But I began to suspect that Murphy's Law was really the world's expression for the mysterious problems and interferences caused by the devil's dark forces. Our beliefs were soon to be confirmed when something happened that was so amazing that we had difficulty believing it was real.

We reassembled the engine and got it started without any difficulty. After letting it run for a while, we stopped it to make some minor adjustments. However, when we tried again it wouldn't start. We checked everything we could think of, including the timing which was right on. But the car still wouldn't start. We were tired and needed a break so we went into the house for a cup of coffee and prayer.

After about fifteen minutes, we went back out to the garage. I was about to close the hood when Frank said casually, "Let's check the firing sequence again." We did and found that the No. 1 cylinder was incorrectly connected to the No. 8 spark plug. As I was about to correct it, I looked at the other connections and could hardly believe my eyes. All the wires were connected wrong. They seemed to be in an entirely random sequence. The specified firing sequence is 1-5-4-2-6-3-7-8. The actual sequence was 8-4-5-7-3-6-2-1.

There would have been no issue if only two wires were interchanged. But not a single wire was in its correct position. It became even more puzzling when I considered how habitually careful I had always been when reassembling those wires. It was always my habit to double check their positions since I realized how vital the correct sequence is to the operation of the car. We wondered if anyone else could have deliberately changed the wires. But that was impossible. There was no way. It was nighttime and the garage doors were closed. No one could have gotten in during our fifteen minute break without our hearing them open the garage doors. We just couldn't explain it on a natural level. The entire experience left us with an eerie feeling.

After we rearranged the wires, the engine kicked right over. What a relief. We made some final adjustments and Frank drove the car home.

Two days later, Frank and I went to a prayer meeting at the Brisson Seminary in nearby Center Valley. We took Frank's car. It drove just beautifully. The engine purred like a kitten and it had decidedly more power than it ever had before. Afterward, Frank dropped me off at my house and drove on home.

As I was about to go to bed the phone rang. It was Frank.

"The car conked out," he said, "and I had to leave it along the highway and hitch a ride home."

"That's a rotten joke, Frank," I replied. "Don't kid about that car. We put too much sweat into it to joke about it."

But Frank continued, "There was a loud noise and a big cloud of smoke came out of the exhaust."

I didn't want to hear anymore. He *wasn't* kidding. I felt sick.

The next morning I got up at 5:00 A.M., picked up Frank and towed the car back to my house. Neither of us said much. Back home we lifted up the hood to survey the damages. It looked really bad. We then removed one of the heads and found ourselves looking into a three-inch hole in the wall of one of the cylinders. The piston was shattered and so were the associated parts. It looked as though an explosion had taken place. Weeks of work literally blown up in a cloud of smoke. We stood there too bewildered and shocked to say a word.

We slowly walked back into the house. I had the hopeless feeling of defeat. I washed my hands and went into prayer, "Lord, help us decide what to do next." As I waited for an answer, the history of the car flashed before me. In less than a year, a car that never gave the former owner problems went through three accidents, a dead battery, a defective starter and timing chain and an engine overhaul. Then there was the snowbank, the two flat tires and the mysterious mix-up of the sparkplug wires. Finally, an explosion in one of the cylinders.

It was clear that this was the final blow. We had to junk the car. Frank came to the same conclusion. This was an extremely painful decision to accept.

We went right out and towed the car to the junkyard. Again, we hardly said a word. I felt as though I was in a funeral procession. It had been a long hard battle. So many things happened in less than a year that they could not possibly have been coincidental.

Now, we are sure that the dark forces of Satan somehow exercised control over that car. Looking back, we remembered that the former owners were, in fact, involved in the occult and we *now* know that this could very readily have placed the car under Satan's control. Had we been knowledgeable in spiritual warfare at that time we would have taken authority in the name of Jesus, bound the spirits, and cast them out. But it would be sometime before we were to become adequately enlightened in this area.

Chapter 9

SICK OF FEAR

A few days later, we were having a discussion about the depth of God's love and mercy—how much He forgives us. We had all been forgiven of so much that we couldn't help but have a deep love for the Lord.

It was like the woman in Scripture who had been a heavy sinner, but had all her sins forgiven by Jesus. As a result, her love for Him was so intense that she washed His feet with her tears and wiped them with her hair and kissed and annointed them with perfume. Simon, a Pharisee, criticized Jesus for allowing her to do this. In response to his criticism Jesus said,

> "Therefore her sins—and they are many—are forgiven, for she loved me much; but the one who is forgiven little, shows little love" (Luke 7:47 *TLB*).

Frank said, "That's why the loss of the car doesn't bother me. Jesus Christ did so much for me that the loss of the car is small by comparison. Besides, I know there's a good lesson that the Lord will show me in time through the entire experience. Perhaps it has to do with trusting Him. In Romans 8:28, He promised to make all things work out right if we love Him. He sure did a great job so far."

Then, Frank decided it was time he filled us in on just how much the Lord had saved him from.

"I was in a real mess before I was saved," Frank began. "I fell into the same satanic trap of drugs that Jim did. It's interesting how similar our experiences were. As you know, like Jim, I had a hitch in the Navy. In fact, I compared notes with Jim once and found we were both in the naval base in Bremerton, Washington, about the same time. Of course, we didn't know each other then.

"But I didn't turn onto drugs in Bremerton. You see, I was assigned to the tender ship, Samuel Gompers. We had left California with the communications ship, Pueblo. Our main job was to accompany the Pueblo across the Pacific Ocean for security reasons. On the way across the ocean, I got to know most of the Pueblo crew very well.

"After we got into the Sea of Japan, we separated from the Pueblo and headed for Japan while the Pueblo continued on its mission. An interesting thing happened the day we separated. Fred, one of my friends on the Pueblo, broke his leg, so they transferred him by helicopter to our ship which was much better equipped medically to handle the fracture. At the time, it seemed like a bit of bad luck, but looking back it's obvious that God had His hand in the situation.

"As you know, the Pueblo was picked up by the North Korean communists and the crew taken into custody. That happened just a day or so after we separated. When we got the news, Fred realized how fortunate he was. If he had not broken his leg, he would have been a prisoner along with the rest of the Pueblo crew. You may wonder what was so special about Fred that God should rescue him in this way. I'm not sure, but he had four children at home and then three days later, his wife gave birth to a fifth. The broken leg seemed like a small price to pay to avoid being a prisoner. Naturally, Fred was happy about the whole thing. I'm sure his wife was, too. Who knows, maybe this eventually led him to salvation."

Frank continued, "Shortly afterward, I was transferred to a destroyer and moved to Hawaii where the ship underwent repairs. My first day in Hawaii, I walked into the barracks to check in and smelled a powerful, but unfamiliar, odor that reeked throughout the room. I asked some questions and learned that it was marijuana—grass.

"Almost everyone seemed to be smoking it. I was soon convinced that it was the thing to do and in a few days, I had my first experience with grass. So many of us smoked it that we decided to take a count, and as I recall, out of the 238 men on our ship, 202 were doing grass or some other kind of drug.

"I soon became so reckless with it that I almost got busted. At the time, I couldn't figure out how I got away with it. But now I think I understand. God was protecting me. After a while grass no longer gave me satisfaction so I went into some of the harder stuff.

"It wasn't until I got out of the Navy that I began to use really hard drugs. By that time, the drug scene was pretty heavy in Bethlehem. I soon got in with all the guys doing drugs—Larry Hatch, Dave Roberts, Carl Hammer, Gil Branci, Stan Mengel, Dick Varine, Sid Hodak and others.

"I remember when I first met Jim (i.e. Jim Priolo). He was clean at the time. In fact, he was the only one in the whole gang who was clean. He had been through so much misery in the drug scene before that he wanted no more of it. Instead he became a crusader, trying to convince all of us how dangerous drugs were. But as you know, instead of convincing us, he got trapped and turned on worse than ever.

"I continued to go deeper into drugs until one weekend when it almost killed me. I went to a rock festival one summer in Atlantic City and Gil Branci started me on shooting 'speed' (amphetamines). I shot enough 'speed' that weekend to kill myself twice over. In fact, I was so irrational I was shooting it right out in the open, completely unconcerned about the law. But somehow, God saved me from the law and from death.

"After I got back home, I started dating Gail and soon fell in love with her. When she learned I was on the hard stuff, she was so upset that she gave me an ultimatum that either I give up drugs or her. Thank God that I really loved her because I never touched the hard stuff again. I was sure glad of that because shortly afterward, Larry Hatch died of an overdose and then Dave Roberts committed suicide.

"Meantime, I went back to grass, rationalizing that it was safe. The truth was that I was hooked on it and there's no safety in being hooked on anything—no matter what it is!

"Then the following spring something happened to you. At the time, I was a little afraid of you. I figured you didn't like me very much, but suddenly you seemed to be a great guy. Then a couple weeks later, the same kind of dramatic change came over Jim. I thought Jim was so badly hooked that there was no hope for him. So whatever happened to him to make such a change had to be for real.

"I told Gail that whatever happened to Dad and Jim, I wanted it. Gail did, too. We were both sick of the kind of life we were living. Drugs weren't the answer. I was sick of being in a constant state of fear—fear of getting busted, fear of not being able to get the grass, fear of losing my job again. You remember, I had thirteen jobs in one year and lost them all.

"So I grabbed onto Jim and said, 'I've got to have what you have, Jim. What must I do?' Jim was only too glad to help. He took Gail and me to a prayer meeting where we heard the salvation message and we immediately committed our lives to Jesus."

Gail interrupted and said, "It was really a miracle. The Lord immediately took away those terrible fears. With Jesus, we finally had something to hang on to. We knew that life now had meaning. You have no idea what it is not to be scared anymore."

Of course, I did, but in a different way.

Frank added, "I haven't smoked grass—or anything else—from the day I was saved. The Lord just took away all my desire."

I sat back trying to understand the kind of torment a drug addict must go through. It was difficult to grasp the depths of his suffering and hopelessness. What a pleasure knowing that for both Frank and Jim, that was all dead and buried.

I said, "Frank, I really hadn't known the extent of your drug involvement. In fact, nor did I know that much about Jim's until after the Lord finally broke his habit.

"For a while, I wondered how I could have been so blind. There were so many obvious signs. But now I feel that my blindness was part of God's work to keep me from messing up His perfect plan to bring our entire family to salvation at about the same time. Had I known about your past, I would have forced Gail to break off with you and I would have lost a great son-in-law. But worse, you might have lost your chance at salvation. And if I'd have known about Jim's drug addiction, with my former hot

Italian temper, who knows which of the many un-Christian things I might have done.

"But instead, God's perfect plan brought us all simultaneously to a crisis where we could willingly make a complete—no holds barred—commitment of our lives to Jesus Christ."

Typically, Dottie sat back with a grin on her face.

"OK," I asked, "what is it now?"

She answered, "What do you mean *former* Italian temper?"

Chapter 10

THE SKY SUDDENLY OPENS

With Frank's new found love for Jesus, he lost no time in witnessing to his parents. He expected that once they saw the tremendous change in him, they, too, would drop everything and run with him. But instead, they cut him to the quick. Their total disdain for his fanatic love for Jesus was quite a shock to Frank. He came away completely bewildered.

Subsequently we gathered in prayer for them and felt certain that our prayers would one day be answered. However, two years went by without any signs of success. Instead, their resistance appeared to increase to the point where Frank was ready to give up.

He came over to the house one day with Gail and their son, Mike, very upset. After some preliminary small talk, he burst out with, "I'm convinced my parents will never be saved."

"Is it really that bad, Frank?" I asked.

"Yes," he replied. "I witnessed to them last night—the

first time I really gave them the whole works—a complete testimony on salvation through Jesus Christ. It fell like a ton of bricks. They all but threw me out of the house. Their thinking is so messed up, they'll never be saved."

As Frank continued to relate further details of their discussion, we occasionally interrupted with words of hope and gradually he calmed down.

Then I suggested that we pray once again for his parents. Frank agreed and he sat in proxy for them. We laid hands on Frank and prayed for their salvation. Although we had prayed for them a number of times before, this prayer seemed to have more meaning. It also gave Frank renewed faith. We knew that God often changed the hardest of hearts, drawing men to Him. He could certainly do it with Frank's parents.

Four or five days later, Gail called. She sounded troubled. "Frank's mother is seriously ill," she said. "They took her to the hospital today. Please pray for her."

During the next two weeks, her condition deteriorated so much that her skin turned a dark yellow giving the appearance of approaching death. She looked so bad that when Frank's aunt saw her, she quickly called Frank and advised him not to visit his mother for fear that the shock of seeing her under this death mask would be too great.

Frank's father was taking it very badly. He had been watching day after day as her condition continued to get progressively worse. He was afraid that in a short time she would surely be dead. The doctors, unable to diagnose the problem, went ahead to perform an exploratory operation. In the meantime, we all continued to pray for her.

The day after the operation was gloomy and overcast, matching the despair of the situation. Frank's father had reached a crisis point. He went into his bedroom, fell to his knees in a deep spirit of humility and repentance, and cried out to God to intervene.

He suddenly felt the strong presence of God—a completely new experience that he didn't understand. But, he was sure that God had heard him and answered his petition and was suddenly full of confidence that God would heal his wife. Then, completely overwhelmed by the reality of God's presence, he asked the Lord to give him a visible sign that his wife would indeed be healed.

While he remained kneeling and staring at the heavy clouds outside his window, the sky suddenly opened up and the sun broke through the clouds, shining brightly for about a minute after which the clouds again closed in, blocking out the sun. He jumped up, wiped off his tears, and began shouting thanks to the Lord for healing his wife.

That afternoon he visited her. The operation was over and she still looked as bad as ever. Nevertheless, Frank's father excitedly kept telling everyone that God had healed her. Some relatives who were also visiting felt that he had lost control of his mind since she looked no better and perhaps even worse.

The next day the doctor reported the result of the exploratory operation. "Her liver is massively destroyed," he said and they could give no confidence of survival. But Frank's father wasn't the least bit concerned. He knew God had spoken to him and there was no shaking his faith and trust in God. In fact, that night he paid a visit to Frank telling him with the greatest joy and confidence that God had healed his mother. Frank related later, "My father had much more faith than I did. In fact, his tremendous faith is what was holding me up."

Time proved that God did, in fact, heal her. Slowly, over the next two weeks, her strength came back and she was discharged. Some time later, she went back for a checkup. The doctor reported that there were no signs left of damage to the liver. Her entire liver was completely healed. So God was glorified through another miracle.

During this period, a greater miracle than the healing took place. Both of Frank's parents accepted Jesus as their Lord and Savior and entered a new life in Him. Praise God!

Chapter 11

LEAVE HIM ALONE

"Leave the devil alone and he'll leave you alone. Every minute you spend talking about the devil is a minute away from God."

This was the kind of advice that I received every time that I brought up the subject of the devil and evil spirits to my Christian friends. But that advice just didn't satisfy me. It wasn't all that cut and dry. It seemed that the closer I walked with the Lord, the greater became my awareness of the influence of Satan and his evil spirits.

Scripture clearly tells us that Jesus spent much time talking and teaching about the devil and evil spirits and casting them out of people. According to Acts 19:38, Jesus went about "healing all who were oppressed by the devil." It's obvious from Scripture that during the period that Jesus walked on the earth many people were oppressed by the devil. It follows that if many people were oppressed by the devil 2,000 years ago, the same thing is true today. The evil spirits didn't simply disappear. They must still be around.

If all this is true, what about me? Am I oppressed by the devil? Is my family? If we are, how can we tell and what can we do about it? What about the experience with Frank's car? Was that a kind of oppression or influence of the devil?

I couldn't find any suitable answers. When I asked these questions I was repeatedly advised to stay away from this area. But I had a lot of difficulty accepting that advice, especially since it had no scriptural support.

Nevertheless, since I was so ignorant of this area, I did try to "leave the devil alone." But, in spite of that, I would soon learn that he would not leave me alone. This came to light one weekend when Dottie and I went to Virginia on a retreat and I left all thought about evil spirits behind. The entire weekend was a real blessing. By the end of the second day, the power of God was so strong that I seemed to float into bed full of the Holy Spirit. No sooner was I asleep than I had a nightmare accompanied by a series of screams that were so loud they finally woke me up, plus everyone else in the room. Then, I quickly fell asleep again.

The next day some of the men commented on the wild screams. I explained, rather apologetically, that I'd had nightmares for many years. However, I added that I couldn't understand why I should have had one last night when I was so filled with the Holy Spirit before going to bed.

Later, after I got back home, I asked the Lord about this experience and he took me back almost thirty years to the World War II era, when I was serving in the Army Air Forces. I was being plagued by extremely painful migraine headaches. No amount of medication would alleviate the pain. At that time, I came across a doctor who used hypnosis to treat his patients, claiming all kinds of success. I went to him for treatment. The hypnosis was unsuccessful in relieving the headaches since they continued as often and as severe as ever. In addition, there were disastrous side effects.

It was right after the visit to that doctor, that I went on a trip to a manufacturer of turbosuperchargers used in aircraft. At night as I lay sleeping in my hotel room, a black cat appeared to be crawling up my bed. It seemed so real that I was filled with terror and began screaming at the top of my voice until I finally woke myself up.

That was the first nightmare that I ever had. But it was the beginning of hundreds of nightmares that were to come back at irregular intervals for the next thirty years. The dreams varied but the end was always the same, bringing such fear that I'd always wake up screaming.

The Lord began to show me that the thirty-year sentence of nightmares was the result of submitting myself to hypnosis. God condemns hypnosis because it uses a power that comes from the devil (cf. Deuteronomy 18:10). I now realized that my involvement with hypnosis had brought me into the devil's spiritual territory, with the result that somehow an evil spirit began to influence and oppress me through nightmares all these years.

Many people believe that a Christian can't be afflicted by an evil spirit. But my experience seemed to indicate otherwise. It was obvious that the nightmares didn't leave when I became a reborn Christian nor when I was baptized in the Spirit.

I thought back to the nightmare that I had in Virginia and realized that there was an important difference about it. I felt no fear when I awoke. In fact, I felt a deep peace afterwards whereas previously I was always left badly shaken. I realized that the presence of the Holy Spirit was so overpowering that night that the evil spriit must have been driven out screaming. The release from that spirit is what brought me the subsequent peace. Yes, Jesus did deliver me from this oppression and I was completely healed of the nightmares that night. Thank You, Lord.

Having proof that I had indeed been troubled by an evil spirit, I wondered if there were other ways in which I could be afflicted. And, as always, I was concerned about my family. Could any of them be afflicted?

I happened to mention my concern to a friend, Glenn. I finally hit pay dirt. He was the first person who seemed interested and unafraid to talk about evil spirits. He was well-read and offered to loan me some appropriate books covering the subject. But suddenly the thought of reading about evil spirits frightened me. The previous advice flashed through my mind. "Leave the devil alone and he'll leave you alone." I backed off and told Glenn I'd like to wait a little while until I became stronger in the Lord.

Christmas season was approaching, our first Christmas as reborn Christians. "This will be the best Christmas ever," I told my family. "We finally know the meaning of Christmas because we finally know Jesus Christ." I was looking forward to it with great anticipation.

The holiday season became so exciting that I spent all my free time in Christian activity. During the week before Christmas I went to church early every evening and to prayer meetings almost every night. One night I even sang Christmas carols throughout the neighborhood, something I had never done before.

December 24th came, the day before Christmas and the bottom dropped out. I got a sudden case of the flu and couldn't get out of bed. "How could sickness hit me at a time like this?" I moaned. "How could I be flying high for the entire Christmas season and then *puff*, lose it all the day before Christmas?"

Christmas Day came and my condition hadn't changed. As I lay in bed, utterly frustrated at my helplessness, I suddenly sensed something that appeared like the presence of death approaching me in the form of a dark mist. It was slowly moving toward me from the foot of the bed. A terrible fear gripped me. As the mist neared my head, I felt like it was beginning to suffocate me. Then it disappeared as suddenly as it came. I was left completely exhausted from the intense fear.

I started to pray, "Lord Jesus, what's happening? What was that mist of death? This could have been the best Christmas ever, but instead I'm so sick I can't even celebrate it." The Lord quickly answered through a verse of Scripture: "My grace is sufficient for you, for my power is perfected in weakness" (2 Corinthians 12:9). But I didn't comprehend the real meaning of that verse and how it applied to me.

The time was approaching for the entire family to gather for dinner. I had always assumed the responsibility of saying grace and really looked forward to doing it on this Christmas. But in view of my sickness, I felt I'd have to forego it this time. However, the Lord assured me that I must go ahead with this plan. I called Gina and told her, "Please call me when dinner is ready. I won't be able to eat, but I'll be down to pray the blessings."

When the time came, I sat at my place at the table and prayed. "Lord, thank You for bringing me and my family together on Your birthday. Thank You for this Christmas, the first one we really understand because we now know that You are at the heart of this celebration." Then I asked God for His blessings on each member of the family one at a time.

As I was praying we felt the power of God fall on us. The presence of the Holy Spirit was so strong that I could barely complete the prayers. Tears of joy streamed from our eyes and our love for one another reached a new depth. Yes, this really was the best Christmas that I had ever had. What better gift than to have Jesus present in such power and glory on Christmas Day. Now I knew what the Lord meant when He said that His power is strongest when I am weak. It was another verse of Scripture that was no longer just theory. Jesus had branded it in my heart on His birthday.

A few days later, as the excitement of Christmas receded and my health returned, my thoughts went back to the dark mist of death. There I was spending 100 percent of my time and thoughts on Jesus, but still the devil attacked me in a most frightening manner. The adage that if I left the devil alone he would leave me alone didn't seem to be holding up too well.

I went back to Scripture and read in James 4:7, "Resist the devil and he will flee from you," and then in 1 Peter 5:8-9, "Your adversary, the devil, prowls about like a roaring lion, seeking someone to devour. But resist him . . ." Both of these verses tell us to resist the devil, not to ignore him. In addition, they are written to believers and, therefore, apply to all Christians. Thus, I could only conclude that the devil's intention to devour Christians means that instead of leaving them alone he is doing everything in his power to attack them and oppress them.

I was sure that the friends who gave me the advice to leave the devil alone had good intentions. They wanted to be sure that we continually kept our eyes on Jesus which I agreed with wholeheartedly. Nevertheless, I felt that after taking all Scripture into consideration a more balanced approach would be to keep my eyes on Jesus Christ, while at the same time learning enough about the devil to determine how to resist him and protect myself from his oppression.

I called Glenn and said, "I'll take those books now." Slowly, I read them, repeatedly interrupting my reading with prayer for protection. I was still concerned that I might be opening a Pandora's box. However, the knowledge I gained from reading Glenn's books gradually dispelled my fears. I felt that I finally broke through the mystery in this area and wanted to expand my learning on deliverance. I bought some books on deliverance written by men like Don Basham, Derek Prince, Maxwell Whyte, Hobart Freeman and others.

It soon became clear that there were indeed many ways in which a person could be attacked by demons. The writers listed symptoms evident in people under attack and needing deliverance. I made a list of the symptoms and found there were quite a few, such things as uncontrollable temper, muttering, chronic fears, and glazed eyes.

Like many a novice, I started to look for these symptoms in my friends. Before long it appeared that my wife, Dottie, showed several of them. After quietly observing her for a few weeks, I became convinced that the symptoms were real and that she was being attacked by evil spirits. She was a prime candidate for deliverance and it was up to me to move in with my recently acquired knowledge on deliverance and set her free from all oppression.

This was all well and good until I tried to talk to her about my plans. What a dreamer I was. How does one tell his wife that she has demons? I couldn't do it, so I prayed for many weeks in the hopes that the Lord would show me when and how to talk to her. But I didn't get a single leading.

Finally, one night, I decided to take the bull by the horns and make my move. I drew Dottie into a private conversation and started to explain as calmly as I could what I had learned about deliverance. As soon as I started I felt a tremendous amount of resistance in the air. This whole thing was much more difficult than I had anticipated. But I forged ahead.

When I was through with all the preliminary explanations, I said, "The point is I'd like to pray over you for deliverance."

In case she previously had any doubts about what I was leading up to, she didn't anymore. I waited for her answer. It came without a moment's hesitation.

"Pray for my deliverance? You've gotta be kidding! Do you mean to suggest that I have evil spirits in me! Ha! If anyone has evil spirits, it's you not me!"

How did I get myself into this mess? I thought that it must be the evil spirits fighting back, so I summoned up enough courage to press on. Finally, after well over an hour of talking, she agreed to let me pray over her.

I quickly called my son-in-law, Frank. He had previously agreed to come over to support me in prayer if Dottie submitted to deliverance. The three of us went into the basement for privacy. I put a bucket and towels nearby just in case I needed them. I knew that departing spirits could get pretty messy and wanted to be prepared for the worse. Dottie sat in a large overstuffed chair in a most unusual position. Both legs were bent underneath. As she sat on them and folded her arms across her chest, she looked much like a statue of Buddha, seeming to say, "I dare you to cast out demons."

We didn't flinch. At this point our optimism was surpassed by our naiveté. Nothing could stop us now. We ignored the signs of rebellion and went into prayer. We praised the Lord, pleaded the blood of Jesus and began doing all the things that we'd read about in the books on deliverance. We commanded the spirits to identify themselves. Half an hour went by but there wasn't a single identification. We felt we discerned the names of some spirits and commanded them to come out in the name of Jesus. Still nothing happened. We continued on and on, praying, commanding, and yelling.

After some time, Dottie began to feel sorry for us. Seeing our sincerity, she started to hope that something would happen just to please us. But after an hour there were still no signs of evil spirits. Both Frank and I were tired and hoarse and rapidly losing our voices so we decided to stop.

It was really perplexing. We expected to see a real show of demons submitting to our commands and obediently coming out with all kinds of manifestations. But there wasn't a single sign of demons leaving, not a single cough, not a single scream, nothing, not even a yawn. I was still hopeful that there might have been at least a partial deliverance since I knew that spirits can leave the body without manifestations.

Frank and I then laid hands on Dottie and prayed for spiritual and physical healing and for a renewed infilling of the Holy Spirit. We quietly put everything back in place and called it a day. No one said too much now. Needless to say, we felt somewhat deflated.

However, there was a real surprise in store for us the next day. Dottie could hardly wait for me to get home from work. She was so excited that she could barely contain herself. She started to relate what had happened.

"As I was driving to the store, I began singing in the Spirit, something that I had always wanted to do, but was never able to before today. It came on me suddenly, just like that! I sang in the spirit for about half an hour. Not only that, but as I sang the Lord gave me the interpretation—the entire passion of Jesus Christ. And then on the way back from the store, I went through the same thing all over again."

Dottie was absolutely thrilled because she was finally able to sing in the Spirit. I, too, was thrilled because this was solid evidence that Jesus did deliver her from oppression, since the obstacle that had prevented her from receiving the heavenly language was now removed. Not only could she pray and sing in the Spirit, but the gift of interpretation was also manifested (1 Corinthians 14:13-15).

A lot of things began to clear up now. My thoughts went back a year ago when Dottie and I both were being prayed over for the baptism in the Holy Spirit, and she was thrown onto the floor by an unknown force. At the same time she yelled, "I can't do it. I can't do it." And she started to cry hysterically. None of us knew about evil spirits at the time so we didn't know how to deal with the situation.

But now, a year later, it was clear that Dottie had been undergoing a spiritual battle that prevented her from receiving the fullness of the baptism in the Holy Spirit. Now that she was set free she did receive this blessing, the confirming sign of tongues. Thank You, Jesus.

Chapter 12

HE WILL FLEE FROM YOU

We were moving into our second year in the Lord now. Our family prayer meetings were weekly highlights. We had been holding them for several months. With the proof of success in Dottie's deliverance, my confidence to minister in this area grew. As a result, we began giving more thought to other needs for deliverance within the family. It wasn't long before they started to become evident.

The first need came one night during a prayer meeting when Kathy, Jim's wife, became terribly disturbed and appeared to be approaching hysteria. She couldn't explain what was wrong. We all quickly gathered around her in prayer. I soon discerned a spirit of fear and cast it out in the name of Jesus. Kathy felt immediate relief so we were sure she was delivered.

In the weeks that followed, other members of the family asked for deliverance as they felt the need. During these prayer sessions, we witnessed the power of God and saw first hand the physical signs of the battle taking place in the heavenlies (Ephesians 6:12).

I became overly excited about this new power and spoke of our experiences to my Christian friends. They promptly tried to discourage my involvement in the deliverance area. Some took great pains to prove that Christians cannot be attacked by evil spirits. But Scripture and our experiences just didn't bear this out. If there were no evil spirits then what was causing the manifestations that we were seeing and the signs of peace that usually followed? We couldn't dispute the Word of God or the evidence. Consequently, we continued to minister in this area.

One night, Pam asked us to pray for her deliverance. She felt a growing anxiety that seemed to be out of control and felt certain it must be oppression by evil spirits. As the family gathered around her and prayed, we witnessed the manifestation of spirits leaving, but she did not feel at peace afterward. In fact, the week that followed turned out to be the most traumatic week she experienced since her rebirth. It became obvious, then, that she had not been completely delivered. Furthermore, we felt that perhaps we had stirred up some spirits that were now causing her havoc.

At the end of the week, we decided to pray a second time for Pam's deliverance. Gina supported me in prayer this time. We prayed for quite a while without success. However, it was obvious that there was a spiritual battle going on within Pam. She looked fearful and appeared to be in an agonizing battle against a mysterious force.

We continued praying, but without success. I felt that Pam could help in the battle by voicing Jesus as her Lord and Savior so I told her to do so. I could see her trying, but she couldn't utter a sound. It appeared as though the spirits were holding her mouth shut.

I said, "Pam, concentrate on Jesus and try to repeat His name after me." She tried but still couldn't get a word out of her mouth. I kept encouraging her. Beads of perspiration appeared on her face. Her teeth began to chatter and finally she began to stutter, "J-J-Jesus." She continued trying and finally burst out with, "Jesus—is—Lord. Jesus—is—Lord. Jesus-is-Lord." She repeated it over and over improving her ability each time. Finally the spirit came out coughing and gasping.

Immediately afterward, Pam yelled, "I'm free! I'm free! It's gone. I'm free!" Then she started to laugh and praise the Lord as another of God's miracles went on record.

No sooner did we get over this experience, than we had a similar one with Gina. When we prayed for Gina's deliverance, she did feel the expected peace, a common sign of a successful deliverance. However, two weeks later, as we gathered for a prayer meeting, we learned otherwise. Dottie quietly directed my attention to Gina. She was sitting at the end of the sofa with her head lowered, sobbing softly. I asked her if anything was wrong. She said, "I can't pray. I just can't pray. I haven't been able to pray all week." Whatever the obstacle it had to be a strong one to keep her from prayer because she had developed a steadfast habit of praying every day.

After some more questions, we all agreed to pray for her deliverance. Several evil spirits were quickly identified and cast out in the name of Jesus. Gina felt immediate release from the oppression and peace again settled over her.

After these experiences with Pam and Gina, we knew that we couldn't depend on achieving complete deliverance after a single session. We had to be prepared for follow-up sessions as the need arose.

Things had quieted down for a few weeks. Then, one

evening, I went up to my bedroom for private prayer. As I prayed, I felt that the Lord wanted me to do something but I couldn't discern what it was. I continued praying but still could not find out what He wanted me to do.

I went downstairs and started to pace the floor. Dottie watched me for a while, then said, "OK, what's your problem?"

"The Lord wants me to do something," I answered, "but I don't know what it is." I thought a moment and then I suggested, "Maybe we should visit your friend, Ann, and talk to her about Jesus."

Sometimes Dottie has a strong way of expressing her disapproval. "If you want to evangelize, do it to your friends," she said, "just stay away from mine!"

I went back upstairs and prayed, "Lord, I know that you want me to do something but what is it?" There was still no answer. I came back downstairs, picked up the Bible and started to read it.

Then the phone rang and I rushed over to answer it. It was Frank, a friend who worked in the same company that I did. He said, "Lou, there are two students at my house from Muhlenberg College. They've been talking about demons and the occult. There may be a need for deliverance." He continued, "I'm not too familiar with this area. Are you busy or could you come over to help us?"

I immediately knew that this was the job the Lord had for me. I answered, "Bless you, Frank. The Lord has been trying to tell me all evening that He wanted me to do something, but I didn't know what it was until now. I'll be right over."

I drove to Frank's house praying in the Spirit all the way. Frank introduced me to Pat and her boyfriend, Roger. They were both Spirit-filled Christians. Outwardly, they appeared normal. I questioned them to learn what the problem was. They explained that there was an occult movement in the student body at college and they were strongly opposed to it. Not realizing the danger, they tried to take action against it one evening by attending one of their séances. Their intention was to fight it from within.

However, their efforts backfired. During the evening, Pat was apparently attacked by an evil spirit and ran out of the room screaming wildly. She lost control of her will, becoming completely incoherent. Roger and some other Christians prayed for her repeatedly over the next few days and she was partially delivered. She was now coherent, but was still undergoing mysterious oppression.

I felt sure that there was more behind this than Pat's visit to the séance. I asked her if she herself was ever involved in the occult. She said that she was. Some years back she played with a Ouija board and she also took part in séances. I said, "This could be part of the problem that you are currently having. When you involved yourself in the occult you moved into the devil's territory. The result could be that one or more evil spirits is now oppressing you because of your past involvement. You should be delivered from all past occult involvement." Then I asked, "Do you want me to pray for your deliverance tonight or should we set a later date?"

"It will have to be tonight," she answered, full of anxiety. "I'll never make it if I have to wait."

Up until now my prayers for deliverance were always supported by members of my family, so I said, "All right, but I'll have to get some help from my family." I then tried to contact some of them, but was unsuccessful. Either the phones were busy or no one answered. After about ten minutes of trying I decided that for some reason the Lord must want me to pray without them. Knowing that I was in God's will, I went ahead in confidence without them and asked Frank and Roger to support me in prayer.

As soon as I started to pray, an evil spirit spoke through Pat and said, "Uh-oh, I'm getting out of here." At the same time, Pat tried to get up to leave, but Roger held on to her. I asked Pat to renounce her involvement in each area of the occult, one by one, and I prayed for her deliverance from them. Then Pat said that she suddenly became ice cold and her heart started beating at a high rate of speed. It was apparent that this was being caused by an evil spirit. Frank quickly got a blanket and threw it over her.

I said, "Spirit, I command you to identify yourself in the name of Jesus." The spirit identified himself as "Fear." I then commanded the spirit of fear to come out in the name of Jesus. The spirit answered, "No." I repeated the command a number of times. Finally, without any manifestation, the spirit left. Pat said, "It's gone. I'm not afraid anymore." Her heart immediately returned to normal and the coldness left. I then prayed for a healing and infilling of the Holy Spirit which is the practice that we usually followed. There was such a spirit of joy that we all began praising the Lord and thanking Him for the deliverance.

We continued to minister in the deliverance area as the need arose. And it arose quite frequently. My records show that over a two month period we prayed for deliverance on an average of twice a week.

Then the enemy started a counterattack. It began one evening after a long, tiring deliverance session for a friend. I felt washed out and started to develop a headache. It became progressively worse over the next two days until I finally had to confine myself to bed.

During the early evening of the second day, I decided I just had to have prayer. I dragged myself out of bed, went downstairs and asked Dottie to pray for me. She looked at me with a kind of disbelief. I didn't think of it at the time, but this was the first time that I had asked anyone to pray for me. I simply never felt the need to ask anyone for prayer before. However, because of this, my request came as a shock to Dottie who later confessed, "I felt like Billy Graham himself was asking me for prayers."

I was too sick to sense her reaction. I only knew that I needed prayer badly. Dottie finally laid hands on me and must have prayed very quietly. In fact, it was so quiet that I didn't hear a word and really wondered if she were praying at all. I went back to bed feeling no better.

The thought then came to me that I needed not only prayers, but in fact deliverance. I considered having my daughter, Pam, and my son-in-law, Frank, pray for me. They were always so strong in supporting me when we prayed for others. Perhaps I should call them. But in my weakened condition that small task appeared too gigantic for me to handle. I just couldn't seem to muster up enough strength to do so. But God was completely aware of my needs and was about to answer me.

In a short while, to my surprise, I heard Frank and Gail as they walked into the house. I struggled out of bed again and went downstairs and said, "Frank, I don't feel too well. Would you pray for me?" Frank took one look at me and thought, "He sure looks like he needs deliverance." It was obvious that the Lord gave him discernment because he spotted it immediately.

We went right back up to my bedroom. Frank led the prayers and Gail supported him. It wasn't long before he identified a spirit of fear which we were learning was one of the more common spirits. He commanded it to come out in the name of Jesus and it came out crying and coughing. Immediately afterward, I felt the most beautiful sensation, as though waves of healing power were flowing through my blood vessels, soothing my entire body, and pouring new life into it. As wave after wave moved through my body, the headache left.

Frank was about to stop praying when I said, "Don't stop yet. I don't feel that I'm completely delivered." He continued praying but it seemed as though we had reached an impasse.

At this point, God brought in reserve power. Pam had changed her plans for the evening and came over to our house. As soon as she walked in, Dottie told her, "Dad's pretty sick. Frank and Gail are upstairs praying for him." Pam didn't wait for details. Without a moment's hesitation she rushed upstairs and joined Frank and Gail in prayer. As soon as she walked in the bedroom, we felt a surge of spiritual power and knew that success was certain. Pam discerned the remaining spirit and cast it out in the name of Jesus. I finally felt completely free and peace settled over me. Indeed, I was both healed and delivered.

We all praised the Lord. How He brought Frank, Gail, and Pam over at a time when I needed them most was just too much. None of them had originally planned to come over that night. In each case, they "happened" to change their plans at the last minute. Thank You, precious Jesus. All glory is Yours.

Chapter 13

THE BUBBLE BURSTS

Our walk with the Lord was not all peaches and cream. In fact, it was turning into a real dichotomy. While we rode the crest of the waves in one area of our lives, we struggled through the valleys in another. So it was that while we thrilled at the way God was blessing us through such things as healings, miracles, deliverances, and revelations, we were facing confusion and frustration over problems that were stealing into our prayer meetings.

I had started the prayer meetings some eight or ten months back because I was certain that the Lord wanted us to have them. Therefore, I treated them as top priority and the whole family backed them up. We had some growing pains, but they were slight and easily overcome. Most of the meetings were beautifully anointed by the Holy Spriit. However, in recent weeks things started to change. Problems started to grow and multiply to such an extent that there seemed to be a continual spiritual battle during the meetings.

Typical of the problems was Gina's boyfriend, Dave. He chose not to attend the prayer meetings, but he had an uncanny habit of timing his phone calls with our periods of prayer. Those calls were very disturbing, interfering with the flow of the Holy Spirit. I finally solved the problem by taking the phone off the hook before each meeting started. This, however, was one of the smaller problems.

A more serious problem was with my son, Jim, who was really having difficulty in his walk with the Lord. He seemed to be on a roller coaster, up one week and down the next. It seemed from the way he often acted in the prayer meetings that he was losing his interest in them.

At one of the meetings, we were all in a spirit of praise and song, all of us, that is, except Jim. He looked very disinterested. It became increasingly difficult to overlook his lack of participation. Critical thoughts were churning through my mind. "Jim is showing more and more resistance to the prayer meetings," I thought. "He's often absent or he comes in late. Then when he gets here he lies on the floor and falls asleep. In fact, he shows an increasing lack of cooperation." As these thoughts continued I became more and more upset.

It was clear to me that his problem was aggravated by the influence of evil spirits. But I also felt he wasn't doing his part to resist them and stand firm as St. Paul tells us to in Ephesians 6:13. Therefore, I said, "Jim, you should make a real effort to sing along with the rest of us. You're only giving in to the influence of the devil when you don't. He is the one who doesn't want you to sing."

I was sure that the point was put to him so clearly that now he would realize that he was falling for the tricks of Satan and really make a determined effort to cooperate.

I was about to start another song when Jim came back at me spitting fire. "Don't tell me that I have evil spirits.

I'm tired of hearing all this talk about the devil and evil spirits! I wish that you'd talk about something else for a change."

That sure backfired. I didn't expect that reaction at all. What does he mean, "All this talk about evil spirits?" It didn't seem to me that we were spending that much time talking about evil spirits. However, there was no turning back for either of us now. We made a few more remarks and then Jim slammed his songbook on the floor, got up and left the room.

The heat of the argument carried me into a few parting comments that must have sent the demons into a victory dance. Kathy jumped up half hysterical and said, "Stop it! Stop it! If you keep it up, he'll never come back!"

Then everything became unusually quiet and I sat back completely bewildered, wondering how things could get so messed up. It was the first time any of us said a nasty word in any of the prayer meetings. But it was now apparent that these feelings were festering beneath the surface for some time. I hadn't realized that making an issue of Jim's behavior during the prayer meeting instead of talking to him in private was a trick of the devil's to disrupt the meeting. By now it was obvious that I had walked into Satan's trap. The meeting was finished!

During the ensuing weeks, a great deal of my time was spent thinking and praying about the problems in our relationships. I buried myself in the Bible and read books searching for answers. Just how much influence did the dark powers of the devil have on what was happening? Surely there was a spiritual battle going on as St. Paul points out in Ephesians 6:12.

This brought to mind a spiritual battle I read about in a testimony by Maxwell Whyte where he and his wife were attacked by evil spirits when they first became involved in the deliverance ministry. They concluded that the attacks were the devil's efforts at trying to discourage them from further work in this area. Is that what was happening to us? We had certainly been deeply involved in deliverance of late.

Pam suggested that perhaps Jim had a point, that we should stop talking about evil spirits, at least for a while. Perhaps we were putting too much emphasis on them. Between the deliverance sessions and the time we were spending talking about evil spirits, this was possible. But I was too stubborn to give in.

In the meantime, Jim and I apologized to each other and our prayer meetings continued. Shortly afterward, pandemonium broke loose in what seemed like an all out attempt by the enemy to destroy our prayer meetings. It started one night when my daughter, Gail, innocently brought her dog to a meeting. My first thought was, "What is a dog doing at a prayer meeting?" Even before we got started the dog did a mess on the living room rug. Gail cleaned it up under a stream of tears and apologies. Then she tied the dog outside, but the atmosphere for the evening was pretty well set.

The meeting was delayed because Pam and Gina weren't home yet. After waiting half an hour we decided to start without them. Jim immediately took off his shoes and moved into a comfortable position on the floor and closed his eyes.

We opened the meeting with singing which apparently disturbed the dog, so he started to howl. We tried to ignore the noise and continued to sing. Pam and Gina came in an hour late. I expected them to slip in quietly. Instead, they burst in talking excitedly, feeling it was of prime importance to explain that they were talking to their cousin, Louis, about Jesus and didn't realize that they were so late for the meeting.

Admittedly, I was terribly upset, but to keep the

meeting going I tried to keep calm. Some days later, my family told me that I wasn't very effective.

I still felt our family prayer meetings took top priority and everyone should put all else aside to make them successful. Since the Lord led me to start them, I assumed that we were following His will. Little did I realize that I was now becoming intolerant about the situation.

As we continued, Gail sensed that something was wrong with her dog because it was no longer barking. She went outside to check but the dog was nowhere in sight. Only the broken leash remained. Gail knew that the prayer meeting wasn't going too well and was, therefore, afraid to mention it to us. Not knowing what to do next, she took the woman's prerogative in a situation like this and started to cry.

It wasn't long before we heard the crying. As soon as I learned that the dog was gone, I stopped the meeting. Several of us picked up flashlights and went outside to search for him. As I walked around to the front of the house, Gina's boyfriend, Dave, came prancing up the sidewalk looking for Gina. He said that he couldn't get through on the phone and came over to find out what was wrong.

Of course he couldn't get through. The phone was deliberately taken off the hook to keep him from calling. As he spoke, the chaotic evening flashed before me—Pam and Gina late, Jim sleeping, Gail's dog and now Dave. It took only seconds to translate the entire episode into one emotional outburst from me. Dave spun around and disappeared into the night. We soon found the dog, but the prayer meeting was now a lost cause.

We tried again and again to overcome our struggles in the weeks that followed. But the dichotomy continued. God did give us some respite by giving us an enjoyable Christmas season.

As usual we planned to have the entire family over for Christmas dinner. Then, we had a scare on Christmas eve. My grandson, Mike, became seriously ill. The sudden attack brought on a fever of 104 degrees. Gail, called in tears asking us to pray for him. She said she was sure that because of Mike's illness, they would not be able to come over on Christmas Day.

I immediately drove over to Gail's house with Dottie, Pam, Gina and Shelley to pray for Mike. When we got there, he was lying on the sofa completely wiped out, a far cry from his usual fire and dynamite. I anointed Mike with oil and we all laid hands on him in prayer. The Lord's healing hand took over immediately. By the next day Mike was fine and our complete family met as planned for Christmas dinner.

After dinner, we gathered in the living room to exchange gifts. Before we started I felt prompted by the Holy Spirit to dedicate my house to the Lord. Therefore, I prayed a simple prayer: "Lord, I dedicate this house to You to be used for Your glory."

Afterward, I happened to glance at my son-in-law, Frank. He was sitting in a chair with the grin of a Cheshire cat on his face so I asked, "OK, Frank, what's so funny?"

"Open up your gift," he replied, "and you'll find out."

I opened it and could hardly believe my eyes. It turned out to be a plaque with a quotation taken from Joshua 24:15, "As for me and my house we will serve the Lord." I yelled, "That's what I just said when I dedicated the house!" There was a burst of laughter as we praised God in what was obviously a beautiful confirmation that the dedication was indeed a blessing from the Lord.

This seemed to be additional proof that God wanted us to grow into a strong family. There were many Scripture references that I suddenly became aware of. In the scriptural accounts of the Passover (Exodus 12:13, 23, 27) and of Noah and the Ark (Genesis 8:16), entire households were saved. This also occurred in Acts 16:31, where St. Paul tells the jailer, "Believe in the Lord Jesus and you will be saved and your household." God confirmed the truth of that last verse in my own household. After I accepted the Lord, He went ahead and saved my entire family.

It became clear to me that a strong family is a powerful tool in God's hands and a powerful weapon against the enemy. But I started to suspect that this was clear to the enemy also because he seemed to be working overtime to prevent us from becoming strong, and with some success.

We continued under enemy attack in our prayer meetings. As a result we no longer felt the presence of the Holy Spirit as we sang and prayed. Without His presence the gatherings seemed futile.

I started to consider the possibility of cancelling them. It was a difficult decision to make. "I would be conceding defeat," I thought. For weeks I strained at the battle going on within me. I rationalized that if I cancelled the meetings, someday we would surely overcome our problems and be able to resume them. Finally, I gave up and just cancelled them. Admittedly, our bubble had burst.

Chapter 14

RUNNING AHEAD

Over the next few months the family went through a valley. We just couldn't snap out of it. "It shouldn't be this way," I thought. "Here we are Spirit-filled Christians, walking with the Lord, praying, fellowshiping, reading Scripture and Christian books and magazines, but still we are being knocked for a loop."

I prayed for help, but didn't seem to get any. Then one day, while I was in the back yard working, I was praying in the Spirit when suddenly a phrase flowed out of my mouth that sounded like Italian words, "*Voi no t'amato*." I thought, "This is unusual. Those words sounded like an Italian phrase meaning 'You don't love one another.'"

But I rationalized that my interpretation must surely be in error since Scripture tells us that we don't understand what we're saying when we pray in tongues (1 Corinthians 14:2). Of course the Lord always leaves room for exceptions and there was an exception the time the Lord gave me the name, Marietta, to identify my sister,

Mary. But I dropped the thought and continued working and praying.

In a little while, the same words came forth, "*Voi no t'amato.*" Suddenly, an awesome fear gripped me. Hearing the same phrase a second time greatly decreased the possibility of error.

A short while later I heard it for the third time, "*Voi no t'amato.*" By now the fear became so great that I was beside myself. There was no question about it anymore. The Lord was admonishing me. In fear that He might admonish me again I could no longer risk praying, so I stopped. For the first time in my life I experienced, personally, the fear of the Lord, and it was indeed awesome.

Admonishing me through my own mouth left absolutely no doubt in my mind of the seriousness of God's message. It is one thing to hear the Lord admonish me through a soft inner voice that I accepted on faith. But it's an entirely different thing to hear Him admonish me loud and clear, through my own voice. Yes, my fear was staggering. I just had to stop praying.

Over the following days, I tried to understand the full significance of the Lord's disapproval. It was difficult to believe that we did not love one another. True, lack of love in my family was a real problem area before we met Jesus. But from the day that He came into our lives, our love for one another grew by leaps and bounds. I was sure we had this area licked now, and would have really challenged anyone who might have dared to suggest otherwise. The Lord must have known how hard it would be to convince me. This was obviously why he had to use such a dramatic method to tell me.

I started to understand that the reason our love grew by leaps and bounds when the Lord first saved us was because we had so many big external problems that He got rid of quickly. But now, He was concentrating on problems that were more subtle and much deeper and probably more difficult to eliminate.

In view of this, I began to search deeper and soon found that there were hidden resentments that I had been overlooking. I didn't know how we could overcome them. I prayed for God's help and strength.

A few weeks later, while still staggering under the impact of the Lord's disapproval, I crossed paths with a friend, Carl, whom I hadn't seen in several months. I had known Carl for many years before we started our walk with Jesus. The last contact I had with him prior to my conversion was in the Florida Keys. A group of us were on a Scuba diving vacation. We spent most of our time swimming through the coral reefs photographing the beauty of the fish and coral with our underwater cameras. The anticipation of sighting baracuda, moray eels, or an occasional shark or manta ray always added to the excitement.

Carl was one of the older divers, though slightly younger than myself. But in spite of this age handicap, he won hands down for the one with the most enthusiasm and endurance. He loved the sport with a passion, so much so that on the last day he didn't want to leave. We almost had to pick him up bodily and carry him off the boat.

But now that Carl found a new love in Jesus Christ, his energy was being directed into his walk with the Lord. I had previously shared with Carl the many blessings that the Lord was pouring out in my family. That was when we were riding high. "But now Satan has moved in and chopped us apart," I told him. "Things are so bad that I had to cancel our family prayer meetings." I expected Carl to react with some sort of sympathetic comment. Instead he burst out laughing and said, "Praise the Lord!"

Well, I didn't think that that was very Christian at all. But he caught himself and quickly explained that at first he had been slightly jealous of how the Lord had been blessing us, and felt relieved now that we ran into a time of testing as other Christians. Then he added a word of advice and said, "Maybe you're running ahead of the Lord."

Running ahead of the Lord? How could that be possible? I was spending all my free time with the Lord in some way, shape, or form. Then I thought back to the large amount of time that we spent in deliverances. Were we running ahead of the Lord in the deliverance area?

One of the local elders advised me to stay out of the deliverance ministry and suggested that a better way to fight the enemy was to emphasize praising the Lord. But it was difficult to accept that advice. I agreed that praise was scriptural, but so was deliverance. I just couldn't discount the many times that I witnessed release from oppression within my own family after praying for deliverance.

But in spite of all the evidence, my arguments gradually began to weaken. I realized that I was standing alone in my convictions. Jim openly challenged my involvement. Pam seemed to be siding with Jim. And there was Dottie who had been against the whole idea of deliverance from the start and usually refused to take part in our deliverance sessions. I was being forced to reevaluate my position.

One section of Scripture kept coming to my mind and each time it did the message became clearer. In the tenth chapter of Luke, it is written that Jesus sent out seventy disciples to heal the sick and preach that the kingdom of God was near. When the seventy returned they were obviously excited about their success in casting out demons because they said to Jesus, "Lord, even the demons are subject to us in Your name."

Jesus was quick to explain that casting out demons was not the thing to become excited about, but that salvation was the real reason to rejoice, "Behold I have given you authority . . . over all the power of the enemy . . . Nevertheless do not rejoice in this, that the spirits are subject to you, but rejoice that your names are recorded in heaven" (Luke 10:20).

It took quite a lot of soul searching to admit that I was probably as excited about casting out demons as those seventy disciples were and like them I was placing too much emphasis on the wrong thing. I began to realize that Satan was taking my interest in deliverance and causing it to throw me off balance. I had to get back into balance.

Bit by bit I backed off, de-emphasizing deliverance, though reluctantly at first. Then something happened that I now suspect was the hand of the Lord encouraging me in my retreat. One night I was asked to assist in the deliverance of a man named George who was obviously under severe enemy attack. I called my son, Jim, and asked if he would support me in prayer. He agreed so I picked him up with a friend and we rushed right over to pray for George. However our prayers were without success. After four hours of praying, the only thing that happened was that I developed a severe headache. It hurt so badly that I was forced to stop. George was no better off at the end of the four hours than he was when we started.

About a week later I was asked by another friend to help pray for deliverance, this time for a woman. Again I spent some four hours praying without a bit of success. Not a single demon was cast out. She, too, was no better at the end of the evening than when we started.

As I left to go home again, completely worn out, it occurred to me that I was apparently not in the Lord's will in either of these two cases. I hadn't asked the Lord if He wanted me to pray for those two people. I simply answered the calls because I assumed they were good deeds.

After those two experiences, I lost my enthusiasm for ministry in the deliverance area. There was no doubt that, for a novice, I was moving too fast and too hard into the spiritual battles we were fighting during our many deliverance sessions. Like soldiers of war, I had battle fatigue and needed a period of rest and relaxation. Carl was right. I had been running ahead of the Lord and found myself leaning more and more on my own strength instead of His. But Jesus is the Deliverer and I am simply the channel. I had to get back in tune with Jesus and put things in their proper perspective.

Chapter 15

HOW TO BUY A CAR

Pam is our first born. Like most of us she had been on her own path of hopelessness searching for a way to fill that emptiness that is reserved only for Jesus Christ. She, too, longed for peace but failed repeatedly to find it. How quickly she recognized the answer when she saw the changes that took place first in me and then in Jim.

Pam always had a deep love for Jim. It thrilled me to see this but it wasn't without cost. It caused her to suffer in sympathy with Jim's every pain. However, just as she suffered with him she also rejoiced when he came back completely changed after that weekend retreat.

Pam knew immediately that whatever it was that Jim experienced, she also had to experience and as fast as possible. She immediately signed up for the next weekend retreat. It was scheduled four weeks away and would be held in a retreat house in Center Valley.

The days passed ever so slowly. Pam's anxiety grew so much that she felt she would burst. Finally, the day arrived. Pam drove over to my house since I had planned to take her to the retreat center. Taking one look at her I knew that she was very sick.

"Pam, you look like you should be in bed instead of going away for the weekend. Why didn't you tell me you were sick?" I questioned.

"I was afraid you wouldn't let me go," she replied softly. "And I must go."

She was right. I tried to talk her into signing up for the following retreat. But she wouldn't hear of it. By now she was so determined to get what Jim and I had, although she still had no idea what "it" was, that to wait another month was entirely out of the question.

I could well understand her driving desire, so I quickly took her to the doctor for some medication. This delayed us by several hours but I finally got her to Center Valley that evening. Afterwards a number of us prayed for her and by the next day she was healed.

As the weekend unraveled, Pam searched for the "experience" that Jim and I had but nothing seemed to be happening. She kept saying to herself, "Why isn't something happening to me? Why don't I feel anything? If I don't find something soon I'm going to let everyone down. Where is 'it?'"

Then just hours before the end of the retreat on Sunday, she realized what the problem was. She had been fearful that she would have to give up all the "fun things" that she wanted to continue doing. She had been trying to hang onto them. Finally, she yelled out to God, "I'll give up everything, Lord. Please help me find what Jim and Dad have!" Immediately the power of God fell on her and tears poured from her eyes in a continuing stream and they continued to do so off and on for the rest of the day.

When I picked her up that afternoon the tears of joy

were still flowing. She was so happy to have the years of heartache suddenly replaced with the peace and joy of Jesus that she just couldn't stop crying.

The tremendous change that came over Pam when she committed her life to the Lord gave her an insatiable thirst for Jesus. Her life was now completely filled with the study of Scripture, prayer, and Christian fellowship. As a teacher, she soon began holding weekly prayer meetings with the students from school which, over the ensuing years, resulted in many accepting the gift of salvation through Jesus Christ. And God in His love and mercy continued to pour out His blessings on her. So it should have been no surprise when God planned a blessing when Pam needed a car.

Pam's car, a Rambler, was showing serious signs of old age. The body was rusted beyond repair and the rear end was so noisy that it couldn't last much longer. These, along with other signs of deterioration, forced Pam to consider buying another car. But, some serious money problems prior to her salvation had hurt her financially for quite a while. As a result, she didn't want to go into debt again. She had $400 saved so she asked me to help her find a good car for about that amount.

During the next week, we covered a dozen used-car lots but there wasn't anything worth buying for $400. It appeared that we would have to look in a much higher bracket before we could get anything reliable. But Pam was firm about not going into debt. Meantime, we were both in a continuously prayerful spirit, waiting for the Lord's leading.

Finally, we narrowed the prospects down to a Ford selling for exactly $400. We began to consider it seriously. However, it had enough things wrong with it that I felt very uneasy. Nevertheless, it seemed like the "lesser of the evils," so we decided that we would buy it. The car was located in Schnecksville, some fifteen miles from home.

After work, Pam and I set out for Schnecksville. As we drove, I mentally viewed the things wrong with the car and started to have second thoughts about buying it. Still, we continued on to Schnecksville.

It was my habit whenever I went anywhere to select the fastest route. However, this evening, for a reason that I could not explain, I took a longer route than before. Seeing that I changed direction Pam asked, "Where are you going?" I replied, "This is a longer route, but it will still get us to Schnecksville. It will give us a change of scenery."

As I drove I told Pam, "There's a road up a bit where we can turn off the highway to save a little time." But the turn off seemed to come up so fast that I missed it.

I drove on to the next turn off which took us through the small town of Egypt. As we came around a slow curve, I glanced across the street at the town garage and noticed a Dodge parked in front with a FOR SALE sign on it. Without a moment's hesitation, I turned the wheel and at the same time said, "Pam, there's a car for sale."

I drove next to it, got out, and quickly looked it over. It appeared to be in good visual condition. The proprietor came over to us. We asked how much he wanted for the car. He said $375. That sounded much lower than I would have guessed. I concluded that there must be something radically wrong with it so I asked to take it out for a test run. He agreed without hesitation. Pam and I got in the Dodge and drove it onto the nearby country roads. I gave it a severe test trying all the things that I could think of to show up possible weaknesses, but it held up well under every test.

"This car is in excellent condition," I told Pam. "It's in much better shape than many cars we looked at which were a good deal more expensive." We stopped the car. I got out to re-examine it more closely, but only a few rust spots showed up and they weren't all that bad.

I got in again and ran it through some more tests and finally said, "Pam, I can't find a single thing wrong with this car. There's no question that it's a good buy. I can't believe he wants only $375 for it. You know that I'm not in the habit of making quick decisions when I buy something, but I know this is the car for you." Pam was thrilled. She quickly agreed.

As we drove back to the garage, I said, "Pam, I think God led us to this car. Do you realize how unusual it is that we got to see this Dodge. I don't remember ever taking this exact route before. Remember how I missed that last turn off? It was the "mistake" of missing that turn that brought us to this Dodge. Yes, I'm sure the whole thing was God's plan. That car in Schnecksville was only the bait that God used to get us here."

Back at the garage, I told the proprietor that we'd take the car. Then I casually said, "There's only one thing that bothers me. I've never yet paid the asking price for a car. Can you take something off?" After I said it I felt a sense of guilt because I knew that it was worth much more. The proprietor answered, "It's already so low, I'm not making any money on it. You see, I just gave it a complete tune up, replaced the tail pipe and a number of other parts." Then he dug into his files and came up with the bill to prove that he wasn't lying. It showed that the work done on the car amounted to more than $50. Now I felt even worse for suggesting it.

I told him, "OK, make up the bill of sale." He did and when I prepared to sign it, I noticed that, without saying a

131

word, he had dropped the price to $350. I chuckled and whispered another "Thank you Lord." It was just too much!

When we got outside, Pam and I burst out laughing as we praised the Lord. Pam said, "Imagine God being so interested in even a $350 car."

I drove home in my own car and Pam drove hers, the Dodge. I was so elated at how the Lord worked that I began shouting praises to the Lord as I drove. I glanced in the rear view mirror at Pam who was following close behind me. She was doing exactly the same thing.

But God wasn't through yet. He seemed to have just a little bit of dessert. Since Pam's old car, the Rambler, was in such bad shape—really beyond repair—I didn't even think twice about what to do with it. I would take it to the nearest junkyard.

On the following Saturday morning, while the Rambler was parked in my driveway, I began removing Pam's personal things and trying to think out the easiest way to get it to the junkyard. As I was mulling over possible arrangements, a man, whom I had never seen before, stopped in front of my house, came over to me and asked if I wanted to sell the Rambler. I couldn't believe it. I said, "I'm getting rid of it. But how did you know?" He said he guessed because there was no license plate on it.

"Well, it's not worth much," I stated matter-of-factly. "There are a lot of things wrong with it," and I enumerated them.

"Does it still run?" he asked.

"Oh, yes, it still runs."

"How much do you want for it?"

"Give me ten dollars and you can have it. It'll save me the work of taking it to the junkyard."

"It's a deal," he answered quickly. "It's worth much more than that in parts."

He gave me the ten dollars and came back later to pick it up.

As I walked into the house grinning from ear to ear, Dottie asked, "What's so funny?"

"You'll never believe it," I laughed.

"Try me."

So I told her what happened and she sighed, "You're right. I don't believe it."

Chapter 16

DOWN THE DRAIN

Before my rebirth I drank alcoholic beverages, though not heavy by the world's standards. I had given up drinking soon after I met Jesus. However, I still had some twenty-five bottles of liquor on hand that I had bought years before. That sounds like a lot of liquor for a light drinker, but I had built up the supply during periods when I was able to get it on sale. It was more a result of being enamoured with bargains than being enamoured with drinking.

It was now about two years since my rebirth and the liquor was still where I had left it. I started to feel the Lord pressing me to do something about it. I agreed I should get rid of it and I began to consider how to go about it. My first thought was to sell it to some of my friends at a discount. But it became obvious that that decision was entirely out of the will of God. It brought me no peace.

Then I considered working it into a very neighborly act by selling it to one of my neighbors at a fifty percent discount. I rationalized that this would be a good Christian act because of the great price break. But the Lord wouldn't give me any peace on that one either. Then I thought, "OK, Lord, I'll give it to my neighbor free. That will be even more Christian and more neighborly." I could just feel the Lord saying, "You're getting close, but try again."

About this time, the Scripture in Acts 19:19 came to mind where the believers burned their magic books. There were so many of them that their total value amounted to fifty thousand pieces of silver. I quickly got the picture. They didn't sell their magic books to non-believers. They knew that their magic books were evil and opposed to God's ways. Therefore, they had to be destroyed. I knew that since I now considered my liquor to be contrary to God's plan, I must draw the same conclusion. The liquor had to be destroyed. I couldn't pass it on to someone else. Doing that would be perpetuating the work of the devil instead of eliminating it. I, therefore, decided to dump it all down the drain. Once that decision was made, the peace of the Lord came over me. Now I knew that I was in His will because I was really obedient to His leading.

On the first Sunday following my decision, my entire family came over to the house for dinner. Right after dinner, I gathered up all the bottles of liquor and announced my intentions. Then, one by one, I dumped them all down the kitchen sink. As each bottle was emptied, the family cheered me on and praised the Lord. It was an unusual kind of ceremony. We had indeed destroyed the works of the devil.

Chapter 17

ROCK AND ROLL

Talk about valleys. My son, Jim, seemed to live in them. Right after his dramatic rebirth, we were sure that he'd settle down permanently. But on the contrary, he needed constant help in his walk with the Lord. He'd go along fine for a while and then suddenly fall flat on his face. We prayed for him constantly. I tried to counsel with him and minister to him when he hit the valleys, but he'd withdraw into a shell of silence and refuse help of any sort, a throwback from his pre-Christian days. Eventually he would come out of the valleys only to fall right back in as soon as something else would trigger him off.

It was obvious that the battle was a spiritual one as St. Paul points out in Ephesians 6:12. Jim was indeed being attacked by evil spirits. We had previously prayed for his deliverance, but without success. By this time, I had recuperated from my battle fatigue and was willing to minister in the deliverance area again. And Jim's need for deliverance was obviously critical. There was nothing I would stop at to help him and I felt we should try once more to deliver him. Pam agreed to join me so we went ahead and prayed over him.

After about ten minutes, I discerned a spirit of confusion and commanded it to come out. As I did something mysterious seemed to be taking place in my chest. I felt as though it was about to burst with this mysterious activity. Then my body began to twist and tremble in a kind of convulsion. At first, I thought that this had something to do with the spirits that were being stirred up in Jim, that somehow they were affecting me.

I continued praying for a while and then discerned that the problem was being caused by spirits that were attacking me and not Jim. I stopped praying and said, "Something is wrong. I don't understand exactly what it is but I believe that the spirit of confusion that I discerned is attacking me and not Jim. Would you change signals and pray for me?" They did and my body went right back into convulsions again. Jim commanded the spirit of confusion to come out of me in the name of Jesus. It promptly did. The convulsions stopped and once again peace settled over me.

We then resumed our prayers for Jim, but again without success. In the meantime, we decided to direct our attention to the ruler spirit (the one that was greatly affecting his actions) that St. Paul mentions in Ephesians 6:12. We felt that the ruler spirit must be keeping Jim in bondage. After much prayer we believed that the ruler spirit might be a spirit of smoking. Jim did have a strong smoking habit. In fact, he tried to quit several times in the past but just couldn't seem to get any success.

We commanded the spirit of smoking to come out in the name of Jesus. But there was no manifestation of it leaving. It became apparent that we were completely unsuccessful since Jim stopped for only a day and was then immediately drawn right back into the habit.

Over the following weeks, as we continued to pray for Jim, the Lord began to lead us to the root of the problem and to the ruler spirit. A light of hope began to glimmer one Sunday when Glenn walked in to give me a new book. Ever since Glenn supplied me with those first books on deliverance, he kept feeding me additional new books, often real gems like this one. It was entitled, *Hippies, Hindus and Rock and Roll* by Bob Larson. Glenn told us that Larson had written that rock and roll music is inspired by the devil and his evil spirits and, therefore, can lead people into bondage.

This immediately drew our interest because Jim was involved in rock and roll music for many years. Jim and I both read the book and found it to be very convincing. We pursued the subject further, listening to a tape by Larson and then reading more of his books. All gave further convincing evidence.

One particular eye opener was Larson's condemnation of the album Jesus Christ Superstar. He explained that this album was inspired by the devil. His explanation was very persuasive. One dramatic point was that the key personnel involved in its composition and production were either professed homosexuals or atheists, so obviously they could not have been inspired by the Holy Spirit. In addition, the album presents Jesus through the eyes of Judas which is further evidence that it could not have been inspired by the Holy Spirit, but was in fact inspired by the devil. We found additional confirmation in George Otis's book, *Like a Roaring Lion* (page 133).

This information rang a bell. That album had crossed my path twice, each time in a very perplexing way. I thought back to those incidents which were both traumatic. Now that I learned that it was inspired by the devil, everything became crystal clear.

My first exposure to the album occurred a couple of years before I learned the truth about it. It was just a few months after my rebirth. A friend, Phil, brought the album over to my house to play it for me. Part way through, my spirit became so distressed that I began to weep uncontrollably and had to walk out of the room. After composing myself, I came back, but the same distress came over me and again I began to weep. I was completely puzzled by my behavior. Afterward, I apologized to Phil for what seemed like emotionalism and I tried to forget the whole scene.

My second exposure occurred a year and a half later, again brought about by Phil. He seemed quite interested in this album and told me that he was planning to discuss it with a church group. He asked me to go over the script and insert the Bible references where they applied so that he could refer to them as he played the album to the group. He stated that my familiarity with Scripture would enable me to find the passages faster than he. At the time it looked like fun so I agreed to do it.

That evening, I sat at the kitchen table reading over the script and inserting the Bible references. But as I did my stomach began to tighten up into a knot. By the time I got into the second page, my stomach hurt so badly that I could no longer continue.

I felt that I was being attacked by evil spirits, so I went upstairs to the privacy of my bedroom and prayed. I questioned the Lord very simply. "Lord, what is it? What is wrong?" His answer came through fast and clear.

"*That album is a mockery to My name. It makes light of My entire purpose for coming to earth. It is a mockery of everything I did to bring salvation to the world. Don't have anything to do with it.*"

Mockery, mockery, mockery. The word kept running through my mind. As I thought back to the script, I realized that the entire production does mock Jesus and does make light of His mission on earth. I couldn't bear the thought of anyone mocking Jesus, the Jesus who brought peace to my household, the Jesus who loved me so much that He voluntarily allowed Himself to be crucified so that I could have eternal life. No, I would not be a part of this mockery. I packed up the script and returned it to Phil with a note explaining what the Lord had told me.

At that time I was not aware that this album was only one of the thousands of songs inspired by the devil. It was no coincidence that Glenn introduced me to Bob Larson's teachings. Not only did they clarify what the Lord had told me previously about Jesus Christ Superstar, but there was much more.

It became clear that the effects of rock and roll music were diametrically opposed to those of Christian music. Just as music can be inspired by God, so also can it be inspired by the devil. Just as the devil counterfeits prophecies, visions, miracles and many other of God's activities, he also counterfeits music. I was so thankful that the Lord gave us a way to know the difference between the true and the counterfeit. Jesus said, "You will know them by their fruits" (Matthew 7:20). Looking at the fruit of the music, it becomes easy to detect whether it's from God or the devil.

The fruit of music inspired by God is readily observable in church and in prayer meetings. Christian songs of praise, thanksgiving, and testimony open the door to God's power. This music is followed by such blessings as healings, miracles, deliverance from bondage, repentance, salvation and an outpouring of God's love that is often absolutely overwhelming.

On the other hand, the effect or the fruit of rock and roll music, the music inspired by the devil, is an open door to the influx of evil spirits. It is often followed by such signs as an outpouring of evil, hatred, violence, killings, riots, robberies and suicides. We read about these signs in the newspaper every day. Bob Larson describes case after case showing that evil does follow rock and roll music.

After reading the Larson books, Jim concluded that he must destroy all his rock and roll albums. He started a fire in his yard and burned each of the albums, hundreds of dollars worth. It was very dramatic. My dumping of the liquor was tame by comparison. We were all excited about Jim's move. But none of us were prepared for the devil's counterattack.

In the days that followed, Jim went into a deep depression, the worst he had experienced since his rebirth. His rebellion was total. He struck out at anything and everything. He rebelled at home. He rebelled in work. The enemy's attack was so severe that one day while he was in his car with Kathy and the baby, he drove at breakneck speeds, toying with suicide. Kathy was in tears almost continually as she called us for prayers and advice.

Our entire family went into prayer. I repeatedly sought the Lord for guidance. Finally, one evening His direction came. It was time for me to counsel with Jim. I prayed in the Spirit as I drove over to his house, trusting that the Lord would prepare the way. By the time I arrived, the Lord had indeed prepared Jim. He was in a very receptive mood.

We talked freely for most of the evening airing out all sorts of things. Toward the end of my visit we moved into the subject of deliverance. Jim said that he realized, now, that his lack of control over the many things that he was doing must be the work of evil spirits. He said, "I know that you prayed for my deliverance several times before, but would you pray for me once more." I thought he would never ask. "Of course," I said. "We'll arrange it for tomorrow night."

We met at my house on the following evening. Most of the family gathered around Jim in prayer, all except Kathy. We felt that it would be better if she didn't join us since her presence might cause a block to Jim's complete freedom to open up during the deliverance session. After some preliminary prayer, discussion and confessions where Jim took a strong stand against the devil, we cast out the spirit of rock and roll in the name of Jesus. Jim's deliverance was finally successful.

We now knew that the ruler spirit we were searching for, the spirit that had Jim bound and was ruling his actions for so long was the spirit of rock and roll. The deliverance was so complete that Jim lost his desire to smoke. A habit that had him bound so tightly that try as he might he couldn't go for more than a day or two without a cigarette suddenly disappeared. We were amazed that the spirit of rock and roll could keep anyone so deep in bondage.

With this new freedom, Jim's thirst for Jesus Christ moved into high gear. He poured himself back into the Bible, prayer, and fellowship and has been running with the Lord ever since.

I thought of the verse in 1 Corinthians 12:26, "If one member suffers, all the members suffer with it; if one member is honored, all the members rejoice with it." We could all say "Amen" to that one. It had been over two years since we were reborn. During that time Jim had suffered all kinds of torment by the enemy and the entire family suffered with him. But with Jim's new release, he was jumping with joy and the whole family was rejoicing with him.

My mind raced back in time again, almost two years,

when the Lord first showed me through Luke 9:38-39 that Jim was being attacked by a spirit that would "hardly leave him alone." Little did I guess that it would take these two years before the spirit would indeed finally let go. I just praise the Lord for leading us to the solution and delivering Jim from this oppression. Yes, all things do work out for good to those who love God and are called according to His purpose (Romans 8:28).

Jim's experience set my son-in-law, Frank, to thinking about his own involvement in rock and roll music. At first he tried to rationalize that he was not as deeply involved as Jim, and perhaps he didn't have to make as rash a move as Jim did by destroying all his albums. He fought and battled with himself for some two weeks before he finally gave in to the Lord and then he, too, destroyed all his albums. Afterward, he felt the familiar peace of the Holy Spirit. We thanked the Lord for clearing up this area for us. Now none of us will listen to any rock and roll music if we can help it.

Chapter 18

ANGELS FROM HEAVEN

One Sunday, shortly after Jim was delivered, he came over to the house for a visit with his family. Their daughter, Lisa, was now ten months old. Kathy was a typical new mother, usually monopolizing the conversation with excited talk about the things that Lisa did. This time, however, she was depressed because Lisa had spent the last three nights crying and screaming. It seemed more than just a series of crying spells.

As we talked, I watched Lisa moving about the room and realized that it had been months since I last saw her smile. I mentioned this to Jim and he agreed that it was true. I felt that we ought to pray for her. Everyone agreed. We waited until she took a nap and then all gathered around her in prayer.

At first we prayed for healing, but then we felt led to pray also for her deliverance. We commanded several spirits to come out and then continued to pray a little longer. I felt that there was still another spirit present but couldn't identify it so I asked the others to pray with me for discernment.

Shortly afterward Jim discerned a spirit of lust. This surprised us—a spirit of lust in a baby? Then Jim added that the Lord had also given him a confirming verse of Scripture. He asked us to look up Ephesians 2:3. We did and read, "Among them we too all formerly lived in the *lusts* of our flesh..." We were satisfied that this was adequate confirmation. Jim went ahead and commanded the spirit of lust to come out in the name of Jesus. Immediately afterward, Lisa woke up with the most beautiful smile on her face. It was a clear sign of release from enemy oppression. We just thanked and praised the Lord for delivering her.

Afterward, we spent some time discussing how a spirit of lust could have gotten into a ten-month-old daughter of Spirit-filled parents. But we could draw no firm conclusions. It was hard to believe it happened, but the evidence was there. Whatever the cause, Jesus took care of the solution.

As a result of this blessing, Kathy burst out of her depressed state and was jumping with excitement. That was part of her nature. When things were great, she'd bubble over with excitement. But when she had problems, she'd fall apart with worry. In fact, she could worry with excitement!

The first time I saw Kathy in this state of excited worry was back in the fall before she and Jim were married. That was the time when Jim had backslidden because of his pending court trial. A number of us had gathered in the family room to pray for Jim. We were all voicing our prayers in a relatively calm manner until Kathy's turn came. She was so full of anxiety and impatience that she said, "Lord, please help Jim and do it right away." I thought, "Wow, she sounds demanding." But I soon learned that the Lord is so full of love that He isn't picky about how we pray. He looks at the intent of our hearts. We humans are the fussy ones who try to limit God.

Now, almost two years later, Kathy was still full of excitement, particularly with regard to Lisa. In fact, Lisa was about to give Kathy the most exciting experience of her life. It was about two weeks after Lisa was delivered that she was moving about the living room in her walker. Suddenly, Kathy sensed that something was wrong. She jumped up and ran to the cellar door. The door was left open and Lisa was at the bottom of the steps. She rushed downstairs. Jim was right behind her. Lisa was still in the saddle of the walker sitting upright. Kathy, who was now on the verge of hysteria, pulled her out of the saddle, but knew instantly that she was safe. All she could say with tremendous relief was "Jesus—Jesus—Jesus." Jim, who was no less excited, grabbed the baby from Kathy, rushed upstairs and on outside with her. There he dropped to his knees thanking the Lord over and over for saving Lisa's life.

It took quite a while before they could settle down and piece together the full impact of the miracle that God had performed. It became apparent that the cellar door was inadvertently left open and that Lisa walked right through the doorway onto the cellar steps. The mystery was how she got from there to the bottom of the stairs. She couldn't have tumbled down because the framework of the walker would have made a considerable amount of noise. But there was no noise, only a slight click of the wheels as they apparently settled at the bottom of the stairs. We believed there had to be only one answer. God's angels carried her down the steps to the cellar floor below.

There was a time when I would have rejected the thought of angels interceding in our lives. But during the past two years, we learned much about the spiritual world, the influence of both the angels and the evil spirits. This incident with Lisa was convincing proof of the protecting influence of angels.

As additional proof that "God was here," the Lord left confirming evidence. He seemed to do this kind of thing quite often, adding bits of confirmation to erase any possible doubts. For instance, the manner in which the walker rested at the bottom of the steps. It was obviously placed there carefully with the lip on the framework that encircles it fitted under the bottom of the lowest step. Had it tumbled down the stairs this lip would have had to lay on top of the step and not underneath.

The most glaring proof, however, was that Lisa didn't have a single bruise or bump. Nor was there any sign of damage to the walker. God left no room for doubt that He had indeed performed a miracle. Thank You, Lord Jesus.

Chapter 19

THE GREATEST MIRACLE

There was no question that the drama and uniqueness of Lisa's miracle made it extremely exciting. However, another kind of miracle was in the making.

It was mid-July. Jim, who had been serving as a scout master, was away at a boy scout camp with his troop for the week. While he was gone, Kathy came over for a visit and brought her seventy-one year old Aunt Betty.

While I was still at work, the girls spent the afternoon talking with Aunt Betty and Kathy.

Just before supper, Pam and Gina took me aside and Pam said, "Aunt Betty is so sweet and lovable, but she has a lot of personal problems. We mentioned Jesus to her several times. I know she doesn't know Him, but maybe you could lead her to salvation."

Gina interrupted eagerly, "Yes, she's so nice. She just has to get saved."

"Good," I answered. "Let's hope and pray that we do lead her to salvation before the end of the evening."

As we talked over the dinner table, I agreed that Aunt Betty had a lovable nature. But I, also, could sense the deep anxiety. As yet, I wasn't familiar with her problems. At one point, Aunt Betty said, "You people are so nice and you have such a beautiful house." I thought, "How polite she is." She continued, "I knew as soon as I stepped into this house that there was something different here. I felt surrounded by an aura of love. I never felt anything like that before. That's why I kissed Pam and Gina as soon as I came in. I never did anything like that before—kissing perfect strangers."

I didn't know what to make of it yet, but it certainly sounded nice. As we continued through dinner, Aunt Betty gradually began to unravel her personal problems. She had lived in Florida for quite a number of years. Through a series of circumstances, she turned the ownership of her Florida home over to her son-in-law. He was an alcoholic and his habit caused him to lose the home. On top of this, several times while intoxicated he had tried to kill Aunt Betty. Things got so bad that she finally decided to flee north for the safety of her life. She was now living with relatives.

There were many additional events she added to bring out the tragedy of her aging years and her growing feeling of hopelessness. It certainly sounded as though she had been through much personal grief.

Occasionally, as she talked, Pam and Gina would excitedly interrupt with, "You know that Jesus can solve all your problems." But she never seemed to pay any attention to their comments, appearing almost oblivious to the interruptions.

As we continued through the meal, I said, "Aunt Betty, Jesus loves you, you know. And since He loves you, He wants to help you, if you'll let Him."

She looked puzzled. "But I don't understand. I used to

go to church all the time, but I never seemed to get anything out of it so I stopped going."

"I understand," I replied quietly. "We did the same thing. We—all of us—had a lot of problems. I did, Dottie did, the children and Kathy did. We felt they were worse than yours and we didn't know where to turn. Finally, we learned the truth about Jesus, how much He loves us, how God sent Him to sacrifice His life for us so that we could be freed from sin and have eternal life."

"You see," I continued, "Jesus loved us so much that He was willing to die for us. It's just too much for me to understand. How much He did suffer! I can't even begin to comprehend the combined pain of the thorns in His head, the insults, and the whipping. Scripture tells us that 'They spat in His face and beat Him with their fists, and others slapped Him' (Matthew 26:67). It was only recently that I really started to grasp the added implications of Him not even being able to sleep the night before His crucifixion, the night that He spent in the garden of Gethsemane."

As I spoke, the power of God began falling on all of us there in the dining room.

I continued, "When Jesus was crucified on the cross, through some deep mystery that only God fully understands, He took all our sins, the sins of every person who was ever born or would ever be born. He took all those sins onto Himself and became sin for us. How much He must have suffered! A man who never committed a sin in His life was now experiencing every sin ever committed in the world—all my sins, all our sins. He did it because He loved us so much and knew that through His sacrifice was the only way we could have eternal life. Now all that's left is for you to tell Him that You accept Him as your Lord and Savior."

By now, God's power had become so strong that I had

151

difficulty continuing. Aunt Betty said, "But how could I accept Jesus? I don't deserve Him. I'm just not good enough. I don't even go to church anymore."

I smiled. It was such a common feeling. I said, "You're right, Aunt Betty. You're not good enough—nor am I—nor any of us. But Jesus doesn't ask any of us to become good enough first. He loves us just as we are."

There were a few moments of silence. Then Aunt Betty cried, "Oh, Jesus, I want You to come into my life."

Almost in unison, we all jumped up, encircled Aunt Betty, and laid hands on her in prayer, praising the Lord for this, the greatest of all miracles—the miracle of eternal life through Christ Jesus. Tears flowed down her cheeks telling us that Jesus had indeed come into her heart. The power of God was so strong that we sang and praised the Lord for more than an hour afterward. Our worshiping was interrupted occasionally by comments from Aunt Betty who would say, "Oh, how dumb I've been all these years. I've got to tell everyone about Jesus. Why did I wait so long?"

That weekend, when Jim got home from camp, Kathy just couldn't wait to tell him about Aunt Betty. Witnessing the excitement of her salvation was such a blessing to us that we all felt disappointed that Jim wasn't there to share it with us. We told him how easy and beautiful it had been, as though God had given us a field ripe for the harvest.

But Jim had his own story. He said, "Don't feel sorry for me. It looks as though the Holy Spirit was busy in a lot of places this past week. Let me tell you what happened at camp."

"One evening," Jim explained, "I sat down with the chaplain and asked him if he had some sort of program for the boys. He said, 'Program? I guess I don't have any program. Why? Do you have something in mind?' I said,

'Why not have prayer meetings after supper?' He acted a little surprised. He never ran prayer meetings before, but he agreed and then asked me to help run them.

"We started the next night. There was a good turn out, about fifteen boys. I read from Scripture and then talked about Jesus and salvation and I gave them some of my personal testimony of what Jesus did for me. They were really interested.

"On the second night, six of the kids asked me to pray with them for salvation and they accepted Jesus as their Lord and Savior. It was a real surprise—so beautiful. I was flying high for the rest of the week. Funny, at first I wasn't keen on going to camp because I didn't know how I could bring Jesus in. But it proves God can use any situation and really comes through in surprising ways."

Chapter 20

BEFORE IT'S TOO LATE

It was September. The schools had just opened and Pam resumed her job teaching the sixth grade in one of the Bethlehem schools. She usually got home from school at about 4:00 P.M., but tonight she didn't arrive until well after 5:00 P.M.

Dottie asked, "What happened? How come you're so late?" And Pam answered, "It's a long story. I'll explain it at dinner." That was par for the course for Pam. Almost everything that happened to Pam was a "long story" and she had to be sure she had our undivided attention before she unraveled it.

While we ate dinner Pam began to explain, "I had a strong urging today to visit a friend at the Muhlenberg Hospital. Well, the visit wasn't all that eventful and I started to wonder why I was there. Then, as I walked through the lobby afterwards, I saw Joanne Rank, whom I haven't seen for years. I asked her what she was doing in the hospital and she said that her father was a patient there. He has cancer. This came as quite a shock to me. I asked if he could have visitors. Then she started to get tears in her eyes as she explained that he was dying and wasn't expected to live more than a few days."

We were all shocked to hear this. We had lived in the same neighborhood with Oliver Rank for some fifteen years before we moved to our present home. I hadn't seen him in perhaps five years. He was in good shape then, but now he was dying of cancer.

We sat in silence for a few moments and then I knew what I must do. "I'm going right over to the hospital," I said. "I've got to pray for Oliver's salvation before it's too late."

"I was praying that you'd say that," Pam said thankfully. "I'm going with you."

We got ready quickly and just before we left for the hospital, Dottie, Gina, Pam and I gathered in prayer.

As we drove over Pam said, "I feel certain now that my urge to visit my friend today was from God. That's how He got me to meet Joanne and learn about her father. I'm sure our visit is God's call." I felt certain also.

When we arrived, we told one of the nurses why we were there. She promptly took us to Oliver's room. The door was closed. Joanne and her mother were in the room visiting with Oliver. The nurse informed Mrs. Rank that we were out in the hall. She came out, and after some preliminary words we explained that we came to pray for Oliver. She seemed pleased, but cautioned us not to stay too long because he had very little energy and visits were taxing. We went in while she and Joanne waited in the hall.

For a brief moment, his emaciated form startled me. But I quickly recovered and prayed for the right words.

"Oliver, I'm Lou Priolo," I said. "Do you remember me?"

He answered softly, "Sure I know you, Lou."

I continued, "This is my daughter, Pam."

He smiled, "Hi, Pam."

He looked very tired but his mind seemed alert.

I struggled to get started, trying to see beyond the drawn look on his face, knowing that the real Oliver was in his soul, not his dying body. Gradually I started giving a brief testimony of what Jesus had done in our lives. Minutes later we were able to lead him to a confession of faith in Jesus Christ. Almost immediately afterward, we were asked to leave for fear of tiring him too much. He died just three or four days later.

The day after the funeral we were again seated at the dinner table. This time, my wife, Dottie, wanted to share something. "I met Pat Gentile today," she said. Pat also lived in the old neighborhood. Dottie explained excitedly, "As we talked, she asked me if I knew that Oliver Rank had died. I said, 'Yes. As a matter of fact, Lou and Pam went to the hospital and prayed for his salvation just a few days before he died.'

"Pat gave a gasp of surprise and tears welled up in her eyes. She explained that she suspected Oliver had cancer for some years. She had tried to talk to him about salvation a number of times, but she had a lot of difficulty. Finally, she decided that she was not the right one to lead him to Jesus Christ, so she began to pray that the Lord would send the right person to him. She had been praying this prayer for the past two years. Now she knew her prayers were answered."

Dottie added, "As you know, I hadn't seen Pat for at least a year. It seems that God brought us together today, just so that we could exchange this information. Pat now knows her prayers for Oliver were answered and it confirmed that Oliver was indeed saved."

Hallelujah!

Chapter 21

A NEW ADDITION

For some time, now, Gina had been going steady with Dave. We all liked him. He was a clean cut, wholesome youth. However, as far as I knew, Dave was not saved. This concerned me because Scripture cautions Christians against being bound with non-Christians. St. Paul explains this clearly in 2 Corinthians 6:14; "Do not be bound together with unbelievers; for what partnership have righteousness and lawlessness, or what fellowship has light with darkness?"

In view of the length of time Gina and Dave were going together, it was possible that they might soon be contemplating marriage. I realized how difficult it can be to oppose a relationship once two people have agreed to take this step. Therefore, it was important that Dave make a decision for Christ before their relationship became more serious.

Several times in our family meetings we prayed for Dave, asking the Lord to bring him to salvation. As

Gina's father, I felt it was my responsibility to protect her from the possibility of an un-Christian marriage. I decided that if Dave did not make a decision for Christ soon, their relationship would have to cease.

Time moved on, but Dave did not appear to make any move toward Jesus. He wouldn't accept any invitations to our prayer meetings. In fact, he seemed to methodically avoid any discussions about Jesus.

As time passed, I became increasingly concerned and began to consider ways to witness to Dave. However, Gina persuaded me not to talk to him for fear that I might come on too strong and turn him off. She wanted to "do it herself" in what she considered a more subtle approach than I would use.

I let things ride for a while, but didn't see any fruit from Gina's subtle approaches. Then, something seemed to be opening up. The elders in the local Body of Christ scheduled a weekend retreat in the Pocono mountains. I planned to attend along with my family. This appeared to be just the right kind of activity to expose Dave to Jesus Christ and lead him to salvation. Besides a weekend in the beautiful mountains should really sound attractive to him.

A month before the retreat, I told Gina I was going to invite Dave to go with us. But again, she was afraid that I would come on with too much pressure and she asked to handle it herself. She went ahead and asked him and he agreed to go. Things seemed to be falling into place. I was now full of hope that he would be led to salvation over the weekend.

The Friday of the retreat arrived. We were getting our things together in preparation for the trip to the mountains. The family was all fired up, looking forward to this time together with great anticipation. Gina called Dave to tell him we were almost ready to leave. From the sound of her voice, I knew that Dave had changed his mind and backed out.

I quickly saw that my plan was failing. My old temper flared and I decided to take things into my own hands. I called Dave right back and said, "Dave, I want you to come right over. I've got to get something straightened out." Gina became upset seeing me so angry and was afraid of what I might say. She ran crying into the bathroom, which had by now become a haven for the girls in times of stress.

I impatiently paced back and forth in the living room waiting for Dave to arrive. He lived close by and was over in a few minutes. I came right to the point. "Dave, Gina is living for Jesus, as my entire family is. Therefore, she is walking in the light. You are not living for Jesus so you are walking in darkness. I've allowed this relationship to continue up until now in the hopes that you would see the light. When you first agreed to go on the retreat, I thought that this might be the opportunity for you to learn about Jesus. But now that you've backed out, the whole picture has changed. I want you to know that if you don't go on the retreat, I won't allow Gina to go with you any longer. The relationship will end. Light and darkness can't go together. You've got to choose."

Dave chose. He didn't go. I suppose I should have known he wouldn't. Even though I was scripturally correct in what I said, my approach was so strong I scared him off just as Gina had predicted. Dottie was quick to tell me that I might have been scripturally correct in what I said, but if the way I sounded was Christian then it was no wonder Dave didn't want to become one.

This clash with Dave brought a spirit of gloom over the entire family. The enthusiasm we had been experiencing for weeks in anticipation of the retreat suddenly went down the drain. We drove to the mountains under a severe strain. I could have kicked myself around the block for being so impulsive and killing the spirit of joy. I thought, "Why didn't I wait until after the retreat? I could have talked to Dave then and probably would have had a better chance of getting my point across. Then I wouldn't have ruined our weekend." But it was too late now.

The entire scene appeared to be a trick of the devil to ruin the retreat and he seemed to have done a pretty good job. I continued under severe enemy attack which caused me to fall into a deep depression.

However, the Lord, in His mercy, came to my rescue as He so often does. When we were all gathered in the fellowship meeting on Saturday, Ann, one of the Christian sisters, discerned my affliction and came over to me and prayed against the spirit that was attacking me. The depression promptly disappeared and I was able to enjoy the retreat activities.

During a break in the program, my family and I gathered in one of the motel rooms for prayer. As we prayed, our thoughts turned to Dave. We all felt a deep compassion for him. We really loved Dave and wanted him to have eternal life, so we prayed for his salvation. We had the reassuring presence of God and knew that He would work out a plan for my daughter's young friend.

When we returned home, Gina remained obedient and stayed away from Dave. In the meantime, the Holy Spirit was apparently working in his heart. After a few days, he contacted Gina and asked to talk about her involvement with Jesus. I gave her permission to do so, but cautioned her to keep the conversation on Jesus. As they talked, Gina held firm in her complete commitment to the Lord. Dave asked a lot of questions about Jesus to clear up things in his own mind. After a few days and a few more conversations with Gina, Dave accepted Jesus as His Lord and Savior. And it wasn't long before he was baptized in the Spirit. We all praised and thanked the Lord. I was thrilled that even though I spoke to Dave in anger, God overlooked it. Perhaps He was honoring my position as head of the family since I had stood on that authority in trying to protect Gina against being bound to a non-believer. I hoped that that was the case. In any event, God came through, true to His word in Romans 8:28; "... all things work together for good to those who love God, to those who are called according to His purpose."

Dave and Gina have since been married. Thus, his commitment to Jesus was God's way of continuing to keep our entire family united in Jesus Christ. Thank You, Lord.

Chapter 22

I AGREE, MR. LINCOLN

I had often tried in subtle ways to drop seeds of faith while at the office. But as yet, it was never anything very dramatic. One summer I saw a potential opportunity to publicly declare God's sovereignty on my job. I was to be the chairman of a symposium to be held at our plant in Allentown. About twenty papers would be presented over a two-day period. Invitations were extended to engineers and scientists from various sister plants scattered throughout the country.

Since one of the duties of the chairman was to give the introductory remarks, it was a perfect opportunity to interject a brief prayer at that time. The more I thought about it the more confident I felt, and finally made up my mind that I would do it. That decision was made five months before the scheduled date.

As the opening day approached, I started to think about what to say in the prayer. But, I couldn't come up with anything that seemed fitting for a group of engineers and scientists. In fact, I started to become uneasy about the whole idea. The enemy obviously moved in and I started to entertain negative thoughts. "As far as I know, no one has previously opened a symposium with prayer," I thought. "My bosses will be attending. What will they think?" Nevertheless, I continued to struggle in search of an appropriate prayer.

I repeatedly talked to the Lord about my problem, asking for help, but receiving no answer. Finally, two days before the symposium, I tried to compromise with the Lord and said, "Lord, I just can't come up with a suitable prayer for this group. Suppose I settle for saying grace at the luncheons?" It didn't take much discernment to know that the Lord didn't care for that idea. But I felt I had no other choice because nothing would come to me regarding the prayer—suitable or unsuitable—absolutely nothing.

The day before the symposium I developed a terrible headache. It was so bad that I had to go to bed early. I had been so concerned about the prayer that I hadn't finalized my opening remarks yet. I decided to set the clock for 5:00 A.M. hoping that when I got up the headache would be gone and I would be in better shape to complete them.

Two hours later, I was suddenly wide awake. My head still hurt, but not nearly as bad. I went downstairs and walked around wondering what to do. I spotted a new book, *Shaping History Through Prayer and Fasting*, by Derek Prince. I had received it through the mail a few days earlier, but hadn't opened it yet. I picked it up and started to read the Preface which turned out to be a reproduction of a proclamation issued by Abraham Lincoln setting aside a day of humiliation, fasting and prayer for the nation.

As I read through it, I felt that there was something more to the proclamation than the theme on fasting. But

166

after I finished reading it once my head began to hurt so much that I was unable to read it again. I dropped the book and went back to bed.

I woke up the next morning at 5:00 A.M. My headache was gone and I went right into my time of prayer. Afterward, I felt drawn back to the proclamation. After reading it a second time, I knew that the Lord had led me to it. It clearly contained the basis for my opening prayer. I quickly pulled out the sections that I wanted and prepared my outline. I was now all set for the meeting. Thank You, Jesus!

As I got up in front of the group and made a few introductory remarks, I moved right into the prayer, saying, "Last night I happened to read a reprint of a proclamation made by Abraham Lincoln on March 13, 1863, where he called the nation to a day of prayer and fasting. In it he said we should 'recognize the sublime truth, announced in the Holy Scriptures and proven by all history, that those nations only are blessed whose God is Lord.' And after Lincoln described how America had been blessed he said, 'We have vainly imagined, in the deceitfulness of our hearts, that all these blessings were produced by some superior wisdom and virtue of our own... we have become... too proud to pray to the God that made us!'"

I continued, "We in our company also have been blessed with much success, and perhaps some of us believe it is entirely due to some superior wisdom and virtue of our own. But I agree with Lincoln that it's because many of us recognize God as Lord. So I want to take a moment to thank Him: Lord—God—Father in Heaven—I want to thank You for the blessings that You have given to our company and I ask You to continue to keep us in Your grace. I also ask You to bless the speakers and the attendees in this symposium, Amen."

I felt a deep peace. I knew that the Lord was listening and was pleased because the prayer was His prayer, the prayer He wanted me to give. Thank You, Lord, for answering my prayer for help in Your way and with Your perfect timing.

Chapter 23

THANK YOU FOR LOVING ME

It was near the end of the work day. I was in my office winding things up. The phone rang. As I picked it up and answered, I heard, "Lou, this is Bill. Am I interfering with anything or could I talk to you?"

I answered, "No, it's fine. Go ahead."

He continued, "I heard that you gave a terrific talk to Frank's prayer group. In fact, I heard so much about it, I'd like you to give it again at the Saturday night prayer meeting at Moravian College."

Bill, an elder in the local Body of Christ, was referring to the teaching combined with a recent testimony that I gave on the subject of love, the love of Jesus Christ. I said, "Bill, I already gave that teaching to several prayer groups and many of the same people will probably be at the Moravian College meeting. They might not care to hear the same message again."

Bill interrupted, "Lou, I heard that the talk was so great that I know they'd all love to hear it twice and even three times. And besides, I've got to hear it myself."

"OK, I'd be glad to give it," I replied.

Terrific! Great! Me? No, not me, but the Lord Jesus Christ. I was the vessel He used, but He is the terrific One. He is the amazing One. Yes, when Jesus does something it is overwhelming because He works with His infinite unchanging love.

Let me go back a few months. My decision to write this book came under a strong anointing of the Holy Spirit and, therefore, I felt highly motivated. I spent every available moment writing, editing and re-editing. As the book started to take shape, I felt that the most important chapter had to be on love. As I skipped from one chapter to another, bringing them to completion, I occasionally came to the love chapter and tried to write something in it, but never got past the title. I seemed to run dry each time I tried.

In the meantime, problems were cropping up again that were exposing a weakness in our family relationships that we still had not overcome. It was difficult to accept the fact that we still had serious family problems. I repeatedly tried to ignore them, in the hopes that they would go away. But the further I proceeded with the book, the more apparent they became. It was almost as though my writing had something to do with exposing the problems.

As the book was nearing completion, I increased my efforts to write the love chapter, but still without success. It was a real puzzle. Here I was, on the one hand, writing a book about God's great work in bringing us together in love, while on the other hand, a close look showed that our family love left much to be desired.

To write a love chapter now would be the height of hypocrisy. As this fact became a certainty, I completely lost my awareness of the guiding Hand of the Holy Spirit and, along with it, my motivation to write. As a result my writing came to a grinding halt. "This book will never be published," I thought. "I might as well pack up my papers and file them away in moth balls." And that's what I did.

Over the ensuing weeks, I resumed my former activities, pretty well putting the book out of my mind. Then one morning, as I went into the family room for my period of prayer, my heart felt troubled, so much so that I had difficulty praying. At the same time, I felt a tremendous longing for the presence of the Lord. I picked up the guitar and started to strum it while I talked to Him.

I continued to strum and talk for a while and soon noticed that my words began to form into lyrics and the chords seemed to blend into a tune. It became apparent that the Lord was giving me a song. This surprised me, particularly since I have no real knowledge of music. In fact, I was a novice at playing the guitar. I could barely get through the basic chords and was still awkward with them. Nevertheless, a song was developing and as it did I quickly wrote down the words.

After a bit, it gelled into a beautiful love song to the Lord, written around my personal testimony. I was thrilled with the fact that the Lord had inspired me to write a song and felt the desire to sing it over and over during the following days. It became apparent that the song had a soothing effect to counteract the mysterious trouble that continued to lay on my heart.

The same day that I received the song, a friend of mine, Harold, called and asked me to give a teaching to his prayer group. I agreed and the Lord immediately gave me the subject. It would be a teaching on love. By now the family difficulties had settled down a bit so I felt no uneasiness about teaching on love. Therefore, I accepted the subject without question.

Based on recent experiences, I knew that since the

Lord gave me the subject to teach on, He would lead me to the necessary material for the message. However, I was learning that He would do this in His time not mine. Since the date of the prayer meeting was a week away, I decided to relax and keep myself open to receive information from the Lord when He did decide to give it to me.

Suddenly it was as though all the forces of hell broke loose within my house. Arguments, bickering, and temper flares came to the surface and intensified as the week progressed. It was the worst week I had experienced since my rebirth. Family love hit an all time low.

I was in a real dilemma. I had to prepare a talk on love at a time when I felt like a complete failure in the entire area of love. For me to speak on love now would be like St. Peter speaking on loyalty right after he denied Jesus for the third time. I couldn't do it. In desperation, I searched for an alternate subject, but my mind drew a blank. There's no such thing as by-passing God. Try as I might, I couldn't think of another subject. There was no question but that the Lord was determined to force me to teach on love, but how?

Time was running out. The day before the scheduled talk arrived, a Sunday, the day I planned to prepare it. I spent most of the day in my bedroom, much of it in prayer. I tried to put the message together, but the harder I tried the more difficult it became. I found myself in a real spiritual battle and didn't quite know what to do about it.

How often I heard people complain, "The Lord is sure dealing with me! Oh, is He working me over!" But I could never seem to relate to that kind of complaint. In the past, to my knowledge, the Lord never dealt severely with me. I felt that when He wanted to teach me something, I simply accepted the teaching. So, I concluded that when someone complained about his sufferings, he was resisting the lesson that the Lord was trying to teach him.

But, I now realized that things were not all that cut and dry. There was no question that I was now being dealt with. My stomach was tied up in a knot. It hurt so much that I couldn't eat. I literally cried out to the Lord for help.

That evening help came as the Lord brought my son and me together in an open discussion. This was probably the most serious problem area. There had been disagreements growing between us for some time.

We started our discussion with great difficulty, throwing out heated accusations and bringing resentments to the surface. But after several hours of discussion, we ended in a flood of tears, repenting and forgiving. We embraced and agreed to try all over again.

This cleansing finally brought a large measure of peace. But I thought it was too late to prepare the teaching on love now. I'd have to call Harold in the morning to cancel it. Somehow, that issue didn't matter anymore. I was tired and went to bed.

However, the Lord wasn't through with me. It was apparent that He knew that my immediate need was rest. So I slept. But at 3:00 A.M. I woke up completely refreshed and filled with peace. I went downstairs to the kitchen to prepare the message. It was clear now that all the obstacles were removed. Thoughts just poured into my mind and in a very short time I had the basic outline for the teaching. I should have known that God would not let me down.

That night, as I delivered the message, the Lord blessed me, the teaching, and the listeners. The comments afterward indicated that the teaching was indeed timely and appropriate for many in the congregation. And Jesus was glorified. Praise the Lord.

However, I left the meeting with mixed feelings. Obviously, I was thrilled at the outcome of the evening, particularly in view of the difficulties I had experienced during the previous week. I was happy that God used this situation to clear up problems between my son and myself. But that situation was only one of the symptoms. The basic problem still escaped me.

When I arrived home, I picked up my guitar and soothed my spirit again by singing the song that the Lord had given me. Then I realized that God had given me the song as an act of mercy. He obviously knew that Satan was planning to sift me so the song was His gift to help alleviate my suffering. It was the only thing that brought me comfort during the past week. Each time I sang it I could feel the love of the Lord soothe my troubled heart. How deep God's love truly is. Thank You, Lord. Thank You for loving *me*.

Chapter 24

A LOVE WITHOUT BLEMISH

Another week passed during which I seemed to be marking time. Then, literally overnight, an acute attack of yellow jaundice wiped me out completely. A visit to the doctor proved that I had a malfunction of my liver that was so bad that I had to be hospitalized immediately.

This was the first time I was ever sick enough to be hospitalized. My health had always been pretty good and I really worked to keep it that way. I ate healthy foods and took vitamin supplements. Exercise was a way of life to me. In recent years, I took up jogging to keep in shape. On top of this, now that my life was committed to Jesus, the Great Physician, I was sure that I would remain in good health. I just shouldn't get sick, certainly never sick enough to be hospitalized. And yet here I was in the hospital, so weak that I could barely walk. The whole picture came as a complete shock. It seemed too unreal to believe.

The doctor quickly filled me in. "You don't have the

common diseases of cirrhosis or hepatitis," he said. Then he hesitated, "You want me to level with you, don't you?"

I didn't like the way he asked. I was afraid the answer was a foregone conclusion.

"Yes, tell me," I said as though I had a choice.

He continued, "It could be cancer, but further tests will have to be made to verify it." Then on two subsequent occasions he repeated, "Yes, you could have cancer. You could have cancer."

I wondered why he kept repeating it. I heard him loud and clear the first time.

He added, "I want you to be prepared so you won't be shocked if the tests confirm it."

"You're so kind," I thought. "So you scare me half to death ahead of time."

Cancer, that sneaky disease. I should have guessed. I always felt that if there were one disease that could get through my healthy living, it would have to be cancer. A cancerous liver meant a high likelihood of sure and fast death, unless God intervened.

For the first time in my life, I was at the place where I could be dying. Not that I was afraid of death. I wasn't, because I knew without a doubt that my future was life eternal with Jesus. But death was never this close.

As I faced the possibility, I thought of the many things that would be left undone. My life's ambition to bring my family into a unity of love would end in failure. Shelley, my youngest daughter, who was now eight years old would have to grow up without a father. And there was my own aging father. Some years back I made a commitment to keep him in my house until the Lord took him home. Now this commitment would be broken. And there were many other things that would go undone.

As these thoughts of failure raced through my mind, I remembered the words of St. Paul shortly before he died,

"I have fought the good fight, I have finished the course, I kept the faith; in the future there is laid up for me the crown of righteousness, which the Lord, the righteous Judge, will award to me on that day..." (2 Timothy 4:7-8). It troubled me, knowing that if I were to die now I could not say that I fought a good fight nor that I completed the course, as St. Paul did. But I wanted so much to walk into heaven like him with the certainty of a job well done.

Soon after I arrived in the hospital, I began praising the Lord. This seemed the natural thing to do, since praise had become a way of life with me by now. Then the Lord impressed on my heart the realization that I was being lifted up by the supporting prayers of hundreds of people in the Body of Christ. I could just feel the effect. In answer to those prayers, God saturated my entire being with His love. At the same time, I knew that whatever the outcome I could trust Him. My anxiety left and I began to feel a deep peace and the awareness of God's presence.

I prayed, "Lord, I want to live. I would like another chance to complete my work on earth. Nevertheless, I accept Your will. I know that with Your great love for me You will do what is best." God's presence was so strong and beautiful that I sincerely felt I was ready and willing to accept His answer, whatever it was. I felt so very close to Him.

The Lord's answer came as a flash message as it often does. In essence, He said, "I'm well aware of all the things that would be left undone. However, you have been brought to the point where you realize that your life on earth can end abruptly. I have allowed this to occur to emphasize the seriousness of my message." Then He assured me that I would live and added what appeared to be a command and yet not really a command, but the solution I had been seeking for so long. "From this day forward, you must love your family with *a love without blemish.*" This was the heart of His message.

A love without blemish? Of course, that was the answer to my basic problem. A love without blemish—agape love—perfect love. In the past, I had read about agape love, but never could quite grasp it. Mentally, I accepted it. But I never understood it down deep in my heart. Now the Lord added a clarifying phrase "a love without blemish." Suddenly the picture became clear and I understood as I never had before. A "love without blemish" was the key that I had been searching for.

I thought of the many references in Scripture to a sacrificial lamb. It was always a lamb without blemish. (Exodus 12:5 "Your lamb shall be an unblemished male . . ."). I never really understood why a blemish was all that bad. But now, I began to see that there was a tremendous amount of significance to it. A blemish, no matter how small initially, can fester and grow and become so big that it can eventually destroy.

I looked for the blemishes in my life and didn't have far to go. They were hiding as resentments deep within me, resentments toward members of my own family. How odd that I should carry resentments toward the people whom I loved most, the members of my family, whereas I had none for the people outside my family whom I didn't love nearly as much.

It reminded me of the song I used to sing years ago; "You only hurt the one you love, the one you shouldn't hurt at all." How well it applied to me. But why was this so?

Gradually, it started to clear up. During the past three years, as I experienced such things as the power of prayer, the power in deliverance, the power of praise, and insights into the Word of God through revelations, I excitedly shared these with the family as fast as I learned about them, encouraging them to share in those same blessings.

This in itself was fine. But I realized, now, that in my anxiety to see them grow in their Christian walk, my encouragement often came with more than a tinge of pressure. When the family didn't respond the way I thought they should a seed of resentment was planted, a blemish. It always started small, so small that it was hardly noticeable at first. But like all small blemishes, in time it would begin to fester and grow and finally become so big that it would begin to destroy our relationships. Now I knew why my love for my family had to be without blemish. Praise the Lord.

As I lay in the hospital bed over the next few days, the presence of the Lord seemed to cover me continuously. While in this atmosphere of His love He led me to verse after verse of Scripture confirming and clarifying His message.

First, He seemed to confirm my own part of the conversation with the Lord by leading me to Philippians 1:21-25, "For to me, to live is Christ, and to die is gain. But if I am to live on in the flesh, this will mean fruitful labor for me; and I do not know which to choose. But I am hard pressed from both directions, having the desire to depart and be with Christ, for that is very much better; yet to remain on in the flesh is more necessary for your sake. And convinced of this, I know that I shall remain and continue with you all for your progress and joy in the faith."

I couldn't get over how closely St. Paul's thoughts matched my own. There could be no doubt left about what had happened between the Lord and me. Thank You, Jesus!

The Lord continued to speak to me through Scripture.

There was plenty of time to do this. The hospital had a fixed program covering a nine-day series of tests for all patients with sicknesses similar to mine. I had to remain there for the complete program.

The Holy Spirit then prompted me to read two verses that showed me how to keep resentments (blemishes) from growing. "If therefore you are presenting your offering at the altar, and there remember that your brother has something against you, leave your offering there before the altar, and go your way, first be reconciled to your brother, and then come and present your offering" (Matthew 5:23-24).

The Word of God goes on to tell us that we shouldn't procrastinate. If we put this off we are giving the devil a chance to get a foothold in our lives. St. Paul explains this in Ephesians 4:26-27: "Be angry and yet do not sin; do not let the sun go down on your anger, and do not give the devil an opportunity."

If I didn't reconcile fast, I would be giving the devil a chance to get a foothold. The longer I hung on to the resentments the stronger the devil's grip would become and the more difficult it would be to undo the damages.

This all seemed so clear now that I wondered why I had so much trouble seeing it in the past. But that, too, started to clear up. In the past we all really did try to avoid causing resentments, but our entire approach had been wrong. We were so fearful of hurting one another's feelings that we carefully weighed our words before we spoke. We were successful in preventing an immediate hurt, one that was so small that it could have easily been repaired with a band-aid. Instead, we actually caused the very thing that we feared most, the hurt that we were so carefully trying to avoid, by planting a seed of resentment that was so deep that ultimately it required major surgery to repair.

So, after walking with Jesus for some three years, I finally learned this lesson on reconciliation. I remember back when I was about five months old in the Lord. I had been running so fast, spending every free moment either praying, reading Scripture or reading Christian books, going to prayer meetings or just talking about the Lord. Then I heard one of the older, more mature women in the local Body of Christ say that it takes about three years after salvation to really get your feet on the ground and feel stability in the Lord. At that time, I thought, "She sure sounds pessimistic. That may be true of others, but surely not of me. I'm so thirsty that give me another month or so and I'll be there."

How wrong I was. As I continued in my walk with the Lord, I soon started to suspect that she might have been right. Now after over three years, I felt that I'd barely touched the surface and that her statement was in fact optimistic.

As I lay in bed, I learned that I wasn't the only one that the Lord was dealing with. My confinement in the hospital was as much a shock to my family as it was to me. Unknown to me the Lord was also working on them. Frank, my son-in-law, spent most of the first day asking, "Why, Lord? Why did you let this happen to Dad?" As Frank kept pleading, the Lord gave him a verse of Scripture, namely, 3:17. The only problem was that he didn't know which book it came from. He prayed for further discernment, but heard nothing else.

Meanwhile, my son, Jim, was going through a similar experience and the Lord was also speaking to him through Scripture. That night Jim called Frank and said, "Frank, the Lord gave me a verse of Scripture. I'd like you to look it up and tell me how you would interpret it."

Frank asked, "What verse is it?"

"Isaiah 3:17," Jim replied.

Frank almost flipped. He quickly turned to it and read, "Therefore, the Lord will smite with a scab the crown of the head of the daughters of Zion, and the Lord will discover their secret parts" (*KJV*).

As Jim and Frank studied this verse they quickly agreed that the Lord was dealing with the entire family. "Dad's the crown," they said, "and we are the daughters of Zion. The Lord struck Dad with an illness to admonish the entire family so that He could expose the problems that we have with one another." Now they, too, began to search their hearts.

My main concern, however, was with the lessons that the Lord was teaching me since I began to realize that after I understood and accepted the Lord's teachings it would be easier for Him to teach the rest of the family.

I began sharing these lessons with Dottie as she visited me in the hospital. On one of her visits, we discussed the nine gifts of the Spirit that St. Paul listed in 1 Corinthians 12:8-10. I mentioned to Dottie that when I was a baby Christian I had a tremendous desire to be used in all nine gifts and what a blessing it was as the Lord did operate each one of them through me in His time as He saw the need.

Then I shared what the Lord had been teaching me in 1 Corinthians 13, the love chapter. This chapter certainly seemed in keeping with the basic lesson that the Lord was teaching me on love. I found that this chapter took on an entirely new and deeper meaning. As I read lines 4-7; "Love is patient, love is kind, and is not jealous; love does not brag and is not arrogant, etc.," the Lord seemed to say, "Don't you see the strong similarity between this chapter and the Beatitudes?" I quickly turned to the Beatitudes in the fifth chapter of Matthew and read them. Then I went back to 1 Corinthians 13 and back to the Beatitudes again.

Suddenly, I saw that both chapters were basically the same teaching—a teaching on love. In 1 Corinthians 13, St. Paul describes various manifestations of love—patience, kindness, lack of jealousy, etc. This appears to be quite clear. However, I found that the Beatitudes given in the fifth chapter of Matthew are also a listing of various characteristics of love—gentleness, righteousness, peace-making, etc. This is not readily apparent, at first. But careful comparison shows some of the same words being used. I decided to write these down side by side.

IN THE FIFTH CHAPTER OF MATTHEW JESUS SAID:	IN 1 CORINTHIANS 13 ST. PAUL WROTE:
Blessed are the gentle (Verse 5)	Love does not brag and is not arrogant (Verse 4)
Blessed are those who hunger and thirst for righteousness (Verse 6)	Love does not rejoice in unrighteousness, but rejoices with the truth (Verse 6)
Blessed are you when men revile you and persecute you and say all kinds of evil against you falsely on account of Me (Verse 11)	Love endures all things (Verse 7)

Thus each Beatitude is really describing a characteristic indicative of love—the kind of love that can only come from God.

As I continued to read the Beatitudes over and over, I could see that a person who is poor in spirit is one who loves. A person who mourns is one who loves. A person who is gentle is one who loves. With each Beatitude describing one who loves, I re-read each one inserting a love phrase which drove it home.

Blessed are the poor in spirit, for *because of their love*, theirs is the kingdom of heaven.

Blessed are those who mourn, for *because of their love*, they shall be comforted.

Blessed are the gentle, for *because of their love*, they shall inherit the earth.

Blessed are those who hunger and thirst for righteousness, for *because of their love*, they shall be satisfied.

Blessed are the merciful, for *because of their love*, they shall receive mercy.

Blessed are the pure in heart, for *because of their love*, they shall see God.

Blessed are the peacemakers, for *because of their love*, they shall be called the sons of God.

Blessed are those who have been persecuted for the sake of righteousness, for *because of their love*, theirs is the kingdom of heaven.

Blessed are you when men revile you and persecute you and say all kinds of evil against you falsely, on account of Me. Rejoice and be glad, for *because of your love*, your reward in heaven is great..." (Matthew 5:3-12)

Dottie was also thrilled at the beauty of this revelation. After I was done explaining it she said, "Did you get any clarification on the first verse of the love chapter?"

"What do you mean?" I asked.

She then re-read it, "If I speak with the tongues of men and angels, but do not have love, I have become a noisy gong or a clanging cymbal." She smiled and I could tell from that smile that something was churning.

"OK," I queried, "what's your point?"

"Well, you said God used you in all the nine gifts. I

guess it looks like you packed your nine gifts under your arm and clanged your gong all the way to the hospital."

What could I say? She was smiling.

At the end of the nine-day test program, the doctor gave his final report. "You no longer have yellow jaundice. All the tests were negative." Then he added, "There are no signs of cancer. We're not sure what caused your sickness nor how it was cured."

There was no doubt in my mind that the Lord had healed me so I said, "There is one possibility you might have overlooked, doctor."

"Yes? What's that?"

"There were several hundred people praying for me and it's just possible that God answered their prayers and healed me," I answered with a calm assurance.

After he spit and sputtered a bit, he replied, "Yes, that just might be possible. That just might be possible."

When I arrived home, I called my family together, anxious to clear up all my blemishes. We spent a time worshiping and thanking the Lord. Afterward, I confessed and asked for forgiveness for all the resentments that existed between myself and the members of my family. As I did, I felt a spirit of deep repentance. But not only me. The entire family did, as tears flowed and God wrapped His blanket of love around each one of us.

As I looked back, I could see that God had been leading me down this path for some time, but I repeatedly fell short of a love without blemish. It wasn't that I didn't try. I did. (Of course, my family had some reservations about that.) I *did* try but I kept stumbling over and over. And funny thing, God always held out His hand and helped me back up each time I nearly fell. A year before the Lord seemed to make it so clear when He admonished me while I was praying in tongues—*Voi no t'amato*— "You don't love one another." At the time I was sure I got the message. But when the tests came, again I failed. It wasn't until I was close to death that I came to really understand. Thank You, Lord, for Your endless patience. Thank You for Your infinite love. Thank You for bringing peace to me and my family.

Chapter 25

A CALL TO THE MINISTRY

With the basic family problem exposed and resolved, the Lord's voice started to come through with increased clarity and we seemed to have a new freedom in our walk with Him. This quickly became evident in Jim's life. For some time he had felt a growing desire to go into full-time ministry for the Lord. He wasn't sure of how to go about it so he was moving cautiously. As the call became stronger he began to pray for some signs of confirmation.

Then one weekend, the Full Gospel Business Men's Fellowship had a convention nearby led by Earl Prickett and Ralph Maranacci. My family attended it.

On the first night, at the end of the meeting, we were preparing to leave when Jim felt an urge to talk with Ralph about going into full-time ministry. He said to Kathy, "Wait here. I'm going up front to talk with Ralph and see if he can clear up some questions about the ministry."

When he got up front, Ralph was busy talking to

someone else, so Jim stood a few feet away waiting for him to finish. Suddenly Ralph made a quick turn, looked at Jim and asked, "Who are you?" Before Jim could answer, Ralph said, "Do you know that the Lord's calling you into His ministry?"

Taken by surprise, Jim stood there for a few moments before he could gather his wits enough to say, "That's exactly what I came to talk to you about." They both laughed at how beautifully the Lord worked. This was just the kind of confirmation that Jim was searching for.

Now, he was convinced that the Lord was indeed calling him. Further discussions over the weekend with both Ralph and Earl seemed to indicate that Jim should remain open to the possibility of going to a Bible school for training and teaching in the Word of God.

Jim immediately began to search out Bible schools. The seminaries seemed to be too heavy on such things as sociology, psychology, philosophy, etc. None of this witnessed to his spirit. He knew that the Bible contained all truth, so there was no point in taking up his time with other subjects. He told me very pointedly that the school he went to had to teach the Bible only or else he wouldn't go. I wasn't too familiar with Bible schools, but that sounded like a big order to me. Nevertheless, he felt confident he would find one.

The better part of a year passed by without any sign of a suitable Bible school. But, Jim's confidence was strong. Then the name of the Pinecrest Bible Training Center in upper New York State began to pop up. He quickly investigated and found that it was a school devoted entirely to teaching and training in the Bible.

When he spoke to me about it, I gave him some words of caution, a habit I had formed from years of practice (and couldn't seem to break). I was very concerned about the big step he would have to take—quitting the job he had had for almost five years and moving his family into an entirely new kind of life. I knew of several such moves that were made in the flesh and consequently ran into much difficulty. So I added, "Be sure you're being led by the Lord."

Then one day, he announced that his decision was made. He would indeed quit his job and go to Pinecrest. He had less than a month left to settle his personal affairs before leaving for school.

The reality of his decision shook me a bit. I thought of how nice things were finally going in the family. And now that we worked through most of our problems I expected God to start using us as a family in some special ways. But with Jim leaving, this would change things—at least it would change what *I* thought God had in mind.

During dinner, I told the family that I was going to visit Jim right after supper to discuss his decision. "I've got to be sure he's following God's direction," I said. "This is a serious decision." Although I didn't realize it, the family could see that I was somewhat apprehensive.

Dottie said, "You'd better wait until you calm down because if you can't go in a spirit of love, you'd better not go at all."

I began to defend my concern. "How is he going to survive? He's got a wife and a daughter to support. And what's he going to do with his furniture and his three cars? What about his outstanding debts? And there are the two German shepherds. He can't take them along. There's too much to do in one month."

Dottie countered with, "You've been telling us that we have to step out in faith, and now that Jim is stepping out in faith, you're all upset."

I had to admit she was right. We continued discussing the subject for the next half-hour. Gradually, my anxiety and fears began to leave. Finally, we seemed all talked out. I called Jim to be sure he was home and left for his house.

Jim and Kathy were waiting for me on their front porch. They were both full of excitement about Pinecrest. As we talked, Jim began to fill me in on the details of his plans.

"Dad," he said, "I know you're concerned, but I'm a lot more concerned than you. I'm aware that if I don't follow the will of God, I'll never make it. I've been praying about this for a long time. I know that there are a lot of people who impulsively quit their jobs to serve the Lord full-time and then find themselves in a lot of unnecessary difficulties. I wanted to be absolutely sure that I was in God's will before I quit my job. So I prayed that if Pinecrest was His will that He would open all the doors and if not, that He would close them. Well, every door has been opened. Things have really been falling into place.

"First, I had promised myself that I would never leave for Bible school until our family relationships were straightened out. Well, as you know, God took care of that since your recent hospital experience. Ever since that door opened, everything else began falling into place.

"Shortly afterward, we received a lot of information on Pinecrest and then went to see the place. While we were there, we learned that they had single rooms and trailers for the students to live in. We felt the single rooms were too small for the three of us, so we agreed that they would have to have a trailer available or we could not accept this school. They didn't have any at the time of our visit, but I just received notification through the mail that they now have a trailer available.

"Then I prayed that the landlord would release me from my present lease. He agreed to do that and promised to return half of my security deposit to boot.

"I sold one of my cars today, the Pontiac, and I think

190

that I can get rid of the Jeep. I'll be keeping the Plymouth. I need about half of my furniture to move into the trailer but I'll sell the other half. With the furniture money and the back pay the company owes me, I'll pay off my debts and we should have enough money left to carry us for a couple of months.

"Then Kathy plans to get a nursing job and I'll work part-time. Really everything is falling into place. The Lord hasn't closed any of the doors. I'm confident that I'm in His will. In fact, I've never had such peace about anything I've ever done before."

I had to admit that I had never seen Jim look so full of the peace of God or so confident in anything. Everything that he said witnessed to my spirit.

Kathy added, "The only thing left is to get someone to take the dogs. We don't want to give them to just anyone. We want to be sure that whoever gets them will really love them the way we do."

I didn't think the dogs were that important an issue, but Kathy and Jim loved them, so they put them in the list of major items.

I left completely satisifed with their decision. As I drove home, I realized that Dottie was right. I'd been trying to teach the family to trust the Lord and to step out in faith, and now that a real lesson in trust presented itself to Jim, I was the one that needed the teaching.

Just days before Jim left, Earl Prickett and Ralph Maranacci were in town running another convention for the Full Gospel Business Men's Fellowship. When Earl heard about the German shepherds, he told Jim he could use them on his farm in New Jersey. Jim and Kathy began joyfully praising the Lord as He solved even this difficult problem.

There was only one open item. The Jeep wasn't sold yet, but it didn't seem to be a real problem. I agreed to arrange to sell it for Jim. So with everything in place, Jim, Kathy, and Lisa left for Pinecrest.

However, no sooner did they arrive than Satan seemed to move in and Jim's faith was put to the test.

The cost of the move and all the expenses associated with transferring into another state, getting settled, registering at school, plus some car trouble, were much higher than anticipated.

In addition, the income from the Jeep did not materialize. I "sold" it to a Jeep dealer. However, through a combination of dishonesty on the part of the dealer and trust on mine, once he had possession of the Jeep, he refused to pay a cent for it.

On top of this, Kathy's attempt to get a nursing job met with considerable delays, leaving no new source of income. So they ran out of money soon after they arrived at Pinecrest and began frugally stretching the food that they had brought with them.

Jim told me later, "I knew that since God brought us this far, He wasn't going to let us down now." As Jim's faith held, God proved that He could be trusted.

Kathy did finally get the nursing job. And there was a bonus. Right after classes started, through a chance remark, Jim realized that he was eligible for subsidy through the G.I. Bill of Rights. He immediately applied for it and within two months started receiving monthly checks. It seemed that the Lord kept this information from coming to his attention earlier to test his faith. "Back at the ranch," we all praised God that Jim's faith brought him through this test in flying colors.

Jim has since graduated from Pinecrest. As of this writing, he, Kathy, and Lisa are in Haiti where they are serving as missionaries.

Chapter 26

A SONG TO ETERNAL LIFE

Over the past year, a number of people I worked with died rather suddenly of either heart attacks or cancer. My first thought, each time I heard of such a death, was whether or not that person was saved. I became increasingly concerned, feeling that I might have lost an opportunity to lead someone to the Lord, perhaps his last chance. I prayed that the next time I would act before it was too late.

The opportunity soon came. Ted, an executive in the plant, was dying of cancer. His name kept popping up in my mind so I began to pray for him. I knew him only on a business basis so Satan tried to use that to disinterest me.

One day, Bob, a fellow engineer, said, "Ted's in pretty bad shape and I feel I ought to go see him before it's too late." This was the kind of nudge I couldn't overlook. I replied, "I'm glad you mentioned it, Bob. I feel the same way. Let's visit him together."

We quickly arranged a visit for the next day. On the

way to the hospital, Bob said, "I understand Ted looks pretty bad so be prepared for a shock."

"Don't worry about it," I answered. "I'll be all right."

When we arrived, Ted's parents were there visiting him. They were about eighty years old and in good health. Bob commented, "It seems so unfair—Ted's parents so old and still in good health while their son, who is much younger, is in the hospital dying of cancer."

Ted did look bad, not at all like the dynamic executive I once knew. He had probably lost all the weight that he could afford to lose and still be alive. It was apparent that his memory was failing since he repeatedly lost his chain of thought while talking.

We stayed for about fifteen minutes. Just before leaving, I felt an urge to pray for him, but I hesitated for a brief moment. Asking to pray with Ted would ordinarily sound so foreign, especially since our past association at work was entirely on a business basis, never personal. But God has a way of eliminating fears.

"Ted," I asked quickly, "would you like me to pray with you?"

He looked pleasantly surprised and answered, "Yes, I'd like that."

As I prayed, I sensed the strong presence of God. Ted's reception to prayer was so full of joy that I knew I must come back and try to lead him to the Lord.

A few days later I paid him a second visit, this time with Roger, another engineer from work, but nothing much transpired. He seemed very distant. Nevertheless, I had a growing feeling that I must find a way to lead him to salvation.

Then one morning, while I was in prayer, the Lord began talking to me about Ted. It seemed that He wanted me to visit Ted with some members of my family. There didn't appear to be anything unusual about that since we were doing more and more ministry together. However, it became very clear that He wanted me to take my guitar along and sing the song that He had given me. This did appear to be unusual. I had never done anything like that before.

Walking into a hospital with a guitar just didn't seem to be the thing to do. On a natural level, it did not sound feasible, particularly because of the receptionist who had stopped me and checked my purpose for each visit before giving me the go-ahead. Nevertheless, I felt sure that this entire message was really from the Lord and I promised Him I'd follow through with it.

That evening as the family was gathered at the dinner table, I said, "I'm going to visit Ted again. I must talk to him about Jesus before it's too late but I'd like some company for prayer support." I hadn't mentioned that the Lord spoke to me about this next visit. I felt that if the visit worked out without my mentioning His message, it would be confirmation that the visit was indeed called by God.

Pam quickly said, "I'd like to go along." Frank, my son-in-law who was visiting at the time, joined in, "So would I."

Trying not to show my excitement I replied, "Great! But you should know that I'm going to take my guitar along."

"Fine," Pam said, "I don't see anything wrong with that."

It felt good to get that vote of confidence. I believed that the Lord's message had been confirmed. We planned our visit for the next day, which was New Year's Day.

It was mid-afternoon when we left. I had a tremendous feeling of confidence that I was in the Lord's will. Pam and Frank did, too, which brought the excitement of anticipating how the Lord would move. We really didn't know how we would get past the receptionist with the guitar. I considered the various things I might say to her, but none of them sounded very persuasive to me.

We walked into the hospital boldly and went up the elevator to the second floor. The receptionist's desk was just outside the elevator door. When we stepped out, the receptionist was nowhere in sight. For a brief moment, I didn't know what to do since I had fully expected a confrontation. But then, I realized that this must be the way God worked it out for us. So, we continued walking to Ted's room.

I suddenly thought, "What about Ted's roommate? Will he be an obstacle to our ministry?" But when we arrived, we saw that, sure enough, God had taken care of that, too. The roommate wasn't in the room. We learned later that he had gone for a walk visiting with other patients.

Ted was sleeping when we walked in. Frank whispered, "What should we do now?"

I whispered back, "I don't know but I'm sure that the Lord is with us. Let's pray."

Frank closed the door and the three of us held hands forming a small circle. We prayed softly both with our understanding and in the Spirit. We continued praying for about ten minutes. A moment after we stopped, as though we were in close tune with the Holy Spirit, Ted opened his eyes, turned his head toward us and smiled.

I walked over and introduced Frank and Pam to him. Our conversation gradually led to why I had brought the guitar. I explained that the Lord had given me a special song that I planned to sing for him. He seemed happy about it so I went ahead, singing softly, so that if possible my voice would not carry outside the room. Pam joined me during the refrain.

When the song was over, there was a hush as we sensed

the presence of the Holy Spirit. It was so easy to talk about Jesus. I began gradually weaving in the gospel message of salvation through Jesus Christ. It wasn't long before Ted gave his heart to Jesus. Tears streamed down his face and he began thanking us over and over for coming. The joy he expressed was beautiful to see. Though he lay there with a body that was wasted away, his soul was alive and rejoicing in the love of God. The presence of God was so strong that each of us automatically leaned over and embraced him.

It was then that I noticed the door had not been completely closed and our singing had carried out into the hall. The nurses heard it, but they felt no desire to interfere. On the contrary, I learned afterward that they actually helped us. When Ted's roommate came back he tried to get in the room while we were still singing, but one of the nurses stopped him and asked him to take another walk until we finished.

I thought, "Well, that was the final touch. Everything worked out perfectly. There could be no question that the Lord directed the entire performance." Knowing He did, we were sure Ted was indeed saved.

Shortly afterward, we got word that Ted died. We felt saddened, but at the same time happy that the Lord reached out His hand in time to give Ted eternal life.

The night of the viewing, I spoke with Ted's wife, whom I hadn't met before. My primary interest was to assure her of Ted's salvation. In the course of the conversation, she said, "Oh, were you the one that had the guitar in the hospital?" I nodded. She then explained that Ted tried to tell her about it, but with his slipping memory he couldn't remember my name. The important thing is that he remembered the only name that really matters— the name of Jesus.

Chapter 27

NEVER TOO OLD

Shelley, my nine-year-old, called out, "It's for you, Dad. It's Aunt Pat." My sister, Pat, called quite frequently. In fact, we talked on the phone almost daily, exchanging tidbits of information on our walk with the Lord.

This time, Pat was really excited. She said, "I now know why I lost my sense of smell and I'm sure happy about it." She was referring to a time some six months back when she had suddenly lost her sense of smell. We had prayed over her several times, but without any apparent success. Nevertheless, Pat repeatedly said with confidence that some day God would heal her.

But now, she had suddenly changed her tune. Instead of confessing her confidence that she would be healed, she was acting glad that she wasn't. At first, I thought that I had heard her wrong. But she repeated, "I'm glad I lost my sense of smell."

I wondered, "Perhaps this has something to do with her father-in-law."

Joseph Cecala, an Italian immigrant, had been a tailor in Staten Island, New York, during most of his adult life. Since his retirement he had been living alone in Staten Island. However, now, at the age of ninety-three, his health was becoming progressively worse, so Pat and her husband repeatedly asked him to come to live with them. He finally agreed and moved to Bethlehem.

But, there was one problem that Pat did not foresee. Mr. Cecala had had a colostomy some years back. He had always been able to nurse himself, changing the bag and cleaning himself as necessary. But with his health rapidly failing, it became increasingly difficult for him to do so. As a result, Pat was suddenly faced with this responsibility.

Pat told me, "You know how I've always been very sensitive about that kind of thing. So when I first realized I would have this responsibility I almost fell apart. But after I got started, I found it was no trouble at all. The unusual part is that the only thing that made me capable of nursing him was the fact that I had lost my sense of smell."

I praised the Lord and quoted one of our favorite scripture verses:

> "And we *know* that God causes all things to work together for good to those who love God, to those who are called according to His purpose" (Romans 8:28).

Pat's phone calls weren't always that full of excitement. "My father-in-law was taken to the hospital today," she said one day. "He's a very sick man."

"What's wrong with him?" I asked.

She answered, "He has bronchitis and a touch of pneumonia. The doctors don't give him much hope. They keep saying, 'After all he's ninety-three years old.' Would you pray for him?"

200

I agreed to, of course, and then said, "Pat, try to lead him to salvation before it's too late. That's really the only important issue. His health is secondary, especially at this late stage."

She agreed.

A week later, on a Saturday morning, Pat called again. "My father-in-law is getting worse. He now has uremic poisoning on top of his other problems," she said. "Please pray for him."

"Have you talked to him about Jesus yet?" I queried.

"I tried," she answered wearily, "but everytime I mention Jesus, he says, 'I always pray to God.' He never mentions the name of Jesus."

I said, "Pat, it sounds very doubtful that he knows Jesus. He needs to hear the salvation message. Let's make a date and visit him together. It'll be more effective. Remember when Jesus sent His disciples out to spread the Word, He sent them out in pairs (Luke 10:1).

She thought a moment and then replied, "Pick me up in half an hour and we'll go right over."

When we entered his room, Mr. Cecala was lying in bed looking very tired and depressed.

"Hello, Pop," Pat said. "I brought my brother along."

He nodded toward me without changing the tired expression on his face. The conversation went slowly.

"How are you, Pop?" Pat asked.

He answered in his strong Italian accent, "I'ma no feela good." He hesitated and then added, "But I liva longa anuf. I ready to die. I joosta donta wanta suffer anymore."

He really sounded sad. We felt a deep compassion for him. Pat said, "Pop, Jesus loves you. He died on the cross for you. You don't have to suffer if you believe in Him."

From then on Pat and I spoke alternately, giving him the Gospel message. At times, we spoke in English and at other times in Italian for added clarification and emphasis. It was obvious that we weren't following any set procedure such as the *Four Spiritual Laws*. Nevertheless, bit by bit, the message of salvation through Jesus Christ unraveled. As soon as he understood the message, he gave his heart to Jesus. Although this is what we hoped for, it took us by surprise.

We quickly laid hands on him in prayer. Pat became excited and said, "Tell Jesus, Pop. Tell Jesus how you feel."

Mr. Cecala raised his arms and began shouting, "Thank You, Jesus! Thank You, Jesus! Thank You, Jesus!" As he did tears streamed down his face and the joy and peace of the Lord moved into his heart.

How beautiful to see this ninety-three year old man raise his hands in praise to the Lord. He wasn't looking for theological proof that this was the proper thing to do. He was simply responding to his heart and automatically doing what it told him.

He recovered enough to come home where he and Pat continued talking about Jesus. Then, one Sunday evening, some two months later, Pat sat on the sofa with him talking about the hope we have of going to live with Jesus eternally. He appeared so enthusiastic as he said, "I pray every day to Jesus and to God." Those were his last words. Minutes later, without a struggle, he went home with the Lord.

Now we knew the real reason why the Lord brought Joseph Cecala to Bethlehem. It was God's perfect plan to bring him to salvation during this eleventh hour of his life. Although ninety-three years old, he was not too old for Jesus.

Thank You, precious Jesus.

Chapter 28

THE MAN BEHIND THE SCENES

As I come into this last chapter reviewing the blessings of the past three and a half years, I sit and ponder, "There are still so many unsaved people in the world. Why did Jesus choose to reach out and save me and my family, while so many others continue in the same kind of torment that we experienced?" Perhaps I'll never know entirely why we were chosen. Certainly it centers around His great love and mercy. But still what about the others? Is it because there aren't enough workers to lead them to salvation? Yes, I'm sure that's part of it. But I believe it goes beyond that—that it really centers around prayer.

So much evidence both in Scripture and practice indicates this—that God's help toward man is preceded by prayer (i.e. 1 Kings 3:9-13, Daniel 9:1-27, Acts 9:11-12, Acts 10:31, James 5:13-15).

Certainly Oliver Rank's salvation was preceded by years of prayer by Pat Gentile. Then there were my children and my brother Tom, my sister Pat, Dave,

Frank's parents, Ted, Joseph Cecala, all with much evidence of prior prayer of which I was a part.

It follows that God's normal way of serving man is in response to prayer. That is, it seems to be one of God's principles, that His work must be preceded by prayer, perhaps much prayer. If God isn't in it, the work won't succeed, certainly not for long.

When I first considered this, I realized for the first time that my salvation, too, must have been preceded by much prayer. I wondered, "But who was praying for me?" Then the truth dawned—the one outstanding persistent voice calling to heaven was that of my own father.

Pop, as we call him, like Daniel, the Old Testament prophet, prayed three times daily. But unlike Daniel, Pop's prayers were primarily for his children.

Completely oblivious of this lone voice calling out to God from his bedroom, my family and I had been struggling through one disaster after another, until God's perfect plan for the salvation of my household became a reality.

During the writing of this book, Pop reached his 97th birthday. His prayers were bearing much fruit. In the past three and a half years, three of his children fully committed their lives to the Lord Jesus plus some fifteen grandchildren. Adding the spouses brought the number to some thirty reborn Christians in the family. On top of this, were the countless others not related to us who were led to Christ by the family members. It was a beautiful testimony of the chain reaction that occurred with Pop's prayers. In spite of Pop's obvious signs of aging in mind and body, he continues, at the time of this writing, to pray three times daily for his children.

As we sat at the dinner table, Pam flipped off the lights and Gina walked into the room with the birthday cake. They collaborated in making this cake for him. Ninety-seven candles were more than they could get on the cake. So instead, they arranged a dozen or so candles to spell out the number ninety-seven.

We all picked up the cue and sang "Happy Birthday to You." Pop sat quietly in his chair at the table with a soft smile on his face, a smile that seemed to confirm the inner peace that had settled over his life during these past few years.

It was good to see this peace that was finally overcoming the loneliness that entered his life when my mother died some twenty-five years before.

Ninety-seven years old meant he was born in 1877. That suddenly seemed so long ago. I thought of God's promise in Ephesians 6:2-3, "Honor your father and mother (which is the first commandment with a promise), that it may be well with you and that you may live long on the earth."

Indeed, my father did honor his parents. Even though I never saw them, there were so many ways that I knew this.

When I was only six years old, Pop went back to Italy to build a house for his parents. I was too young to understand this, but years later I learned the missing details. His parents had always lived in the confined quarters of a simple two-room house. When my father came to America, it became his deepest ambition to return someday to build them a house they could be proud of.

In spite of being burdened with the heavy expenses of raising us—his nine children—he began saving money for this venture, at times working at two full-time carpenter jobs simultaneously.

Finally, he made the trip back to Italy. With the help of his brothers, he laid in a concrete floor and built all the wooden framework, including the roof. After this, he returned to his family in America, but continued to supply money to complete the house. When it was finally completed, it turned out to be a showplace in the small village, giving my father a deep sense of satisfaction. Afterward, he still found it in his heart to continue to send money for their support right up until they died. Yes, Pop did truly honor his parents and now God was true to His Word, giving Pop the long life He promised.

Pop was a carpenter by trade and a good one, well-recognized for his ability, speed, strength, and stamina. It gave me a good feeling, knowing he was a carpenter just as Jesus was.

Although Pop worked hard, he still had time for his children. Occasionally, he took his sons on job sites with him. I remember the time I finally got my chance. I was ten years old. He agreed to let me help nail floor boards in a house he was renovating. I could still see him carrying his long wooden tool box on his shoulder as he walked to the job site and I ran along beside him. He looked so strong and majestic. It made me feel proud to be his son.

He had his lighter moments, too, being famous in the neighborhood for a trick he would repeatedly perform that just baffled us youngsters. He took a needle, held it up for us to see, and then quickly pounded it into his forehead. Seconds later, he would pull it out of some other part of his body. It took a long time before I learned that he had the needle stuck through the surface layer of skin on his thumb. His fast hand movements, of course, distracted us enough to miss it.

The years went by and most of the children got married. When my mother died, he sold his house and for the past twenty-five years had lived with one or another of his children. But he became increasingly lonely, which caused him to become more and more difficult to live with.

Some nine years ago, I had asked him to live with me.

He agreed, but my sisters cautioned me that he would be very difficult, particularly on my wife, Dottie.

I knew this could be true. Nevertheless, I said, "This move gives me a good feeling down deep inside and somehow I know it will be good for my soul." It was almost as though the Lord put the words in my mouth since my knowledge of the soul was terribly vague at the time.

As time went by, my sisters proved to be right. I struggled, trying to adjust to his strong-willed ways. He was particularly hard on Dottie and I found myself continually in the middle of things trying to keep peace between them.

The growing problems between Dottie and me and the children only compounded the difficulties with my father and our disagreements began to increase. Periodically, his temper and mine would flare up and end in a typically heated Italian explosion of words. For days afterward, I would withdraw into a shell of guilt.

Finally, Jesus came into our lives and the revolution throughout the household carried right over to my father. With the peace that Jesus brought to each of us, my father no longer seemed to be a problem. Now, instead of worrying about when the next explosion would take place, I began praying for him and for a healing of our relationships.

Things improved so much that I thought all the problems between us were gone forever.

Then one day, when I was about a year old in the Lord, I came home during the lunch hour. No one was home except Pop. He was sitting in his favorite chair in the living room and looked as though something was bothering him. He said he wanted to talk to me.

As I listened, he began to unload complaints and criticisms that he had been harboring for some time. That had been his old habit, but this was the first time that he had done it since my rebirth. I knew from past experience that this would lead to something distasteful so I tried to change the subject. But, try as I might, I couldn't succeed. He continued in his criticisms and I finally lost my temper and said some things that I wished I hadn't. Then I got up and went into the family room to collect my wits. I sat there feeling terribly guilty. I loved my father too much to hurt him. And yet I did. There was no question, I fell right into the devil's trap. Things had been going so well and I had to go and blow it.

I began to pray and as I did my thoughts drifted to the many years my father spent praying daily for all of his children. I was sure that it was no coincidence that I was the first one of his children to be saved. My father was a priest in his own right and God honored his priesthood. We were living in the same household when his prayers for me were answered. And, God does specialize in saving households (Acts 16:31). Perhaps this is why I had that good feeling down deep inside when he first came to live with me. But, knowing all this made me feel even worse.

It was time to leave for work now. As I drove, I prayed, asking God for forgiveness. I began to realize how wrong it was that the older my father got, the more tormented he became.

No, it just didn't seem right at all. If living a long life is God's reward, then life should certainly not be a tormented one. His twilight years should be happy ones, devoid of suffering. I suddenly sensed that this torment was the work of the devil and that only God could help.

I prayed, "Lord, I know that *You* have kept my father alive all these years and I know that it's not Your purpose to have him suffer. This must be the work of the devil. So, Lord, please keep the evil one away from him and bring him peace during his few remaining years here on earth."

208

As I was still praying, I felt the Lord answer with a tremendous assurance that he would indeed bring peace to my father. Tears came to my eyes as I felt the power of God's love envelope me. It was so overwhelming that it was all I could do to keep the car on the road. It didn't matter, because I was certain, now, that God would indeed take care of my father and bring him peace in the coming years.

That evening, when I came home from work, my father was again sitting in his favorite chair in the living room. I went right over to him, knelt down by his side and asked him for forgiveness.

Since that day a new peace came into his life. God had indeed reversed the trend of the preceding twenty-five years. His peace continues to grow deeper, proving that the tormenting power of the devil was indeed broken.

And so it was that this cycle completed itself. God responded to Pop's prayers for me and then He responded to my prayers for him. Yes, prayer is the key that opens the door.

It seems so many years ago when I first called out to the Lord in prayer, "Dear Lord, please bring peace to me and my family this year." It was the turning point that brought me out of the past and put me into the present with hope for the future.

Past—Present—Future.

The past is gone—the hopelessness, despair and sick stomach feelings; the hatred, resentments and the uncontrolled tempers; the drugs and runaway kids; the nightmares, the fear to live and fear to die—all the things of the past, dead and buried at the Cross.

All of that is now replaced by the present, a will to live in a life full of peace and joy and love in Jesus Christ.

And a future full of assurance that although we will

continue to go through trials, God will always be with us to give us the strength to overcome.

But beyond it all is our hope, our conviction of eternal life with God the Father and His Son Jesus Christ, the Alpha and Omega, Who is, Who was and Who is to come.

Maranatha!

WHEREVER PAPERBACKS ARE SOLD
OR USE THIS COUPON

Pittsburgh and Colfax Streets
Springdale, Pa. 15144

SEND INSPIRATIONAL BOOKS
LISTED BELOW

Title   Price   ☐ Send
                                               Complete
                                               Catalog

_____   _____

_____   _____

_____   _____

_____   _____

_____   _____

_____   _____

_____   _____

_____   _____

Name_____

Street _____

City_____ State____ Zip _____

Suggested Inspirational Paperback Books

PRAISE AVENUE
by Don Gossett $1.50

Praise can change your life! It's impossible to overestimate the power, victory, blessing, healing, and inspiration available to you through the practical application of the principles revealed in this book.

SPIRITUAL POWER
by Don Basham $1.45

Multitudes have received new spiritual power after hearing Don Basham speak. Now you too can have this life-changing experience, just by following the simple steps outlined in this easy-to-read little book.

HOLIDAY IN HELL
by Chico Holiday & Bob Owen $1.75

"If Chico's road from nightclub entertainer to singing evangelist had been an easy one, I doubt that there would be a book called HOLIDAY IN HELL. It's a hard, honest, heartwarming account of two lives in the midst of miraculous transformation, told as they have lived it"...Pat Boone

JESSE
by Jesse Winley & Robert Paul Lamb $1.75

The fascinating story of a true servant of God. Jesse Winley is a man who has been called many things; courageous/stubborn; gentle/firm; daring/influential. He has been sought after—threatened—adulated—feared. But through it all he has lived the vibrant life of a conqueror.

WHAT YOU SAY IS WHAT YOU GET
by Don Gosset

$1.75

Don Gossett reveals how your own words can tap in on spiritual power that will bring you love, joy, peace, happiness, success, and prosperity. You will be amazed to find that WHAT YOU SAY IS WHAT YOU GET.

CHAPTER 29
by Jean Coleman

$1.75

Just a housewife?! That's all that Jean Coleman thought of herself until the exciting day when she embarked on a new adventure of life. Miraculously, she began to live her own 29th chapter of the book of Acts!

THREE BEHIND THE CURTAIN
by Sammy Tippit & Jerry Jenkins

$1.50

"There were the three of us. Surrounded by 100,000 Communists. And the message we were carrying was of life and death importance. How could we reach the ones who needed to hear it?"...Sammy Tippit

FREEDOM TO CHOOSE
by Ernest J. Gruen

$1.75

Have you ever wondered what life would be like if the cares of each day could be lifted? You can be set free to a life of joy and peace—soaring high above the daily mountains you thought you couldn't even climb!

AS FOR ME AND MY HOUSE
by Louis A. Priolo

$1.75

A dynamic story that will bring tears to your eyes as you follow the joys and sorrows of this exciting family. A father of five reveals the Answer that breaks through the generation gap, the communication gap and most of all—the love gap.

DAMASCUS APPOINTMENT
by Jerry Rutkin & J. Stephen Conn $1.50

Jerry Rutkin was a young Jewish boy walking a pathway strewn with the pitfalls of crime and rebellion. His traveling companions were loneliness and despair, his destination—early death. Wearied from his travels, Jerry met Someone new on the "road to Damascus." Suddenly all things had become new!

YESTERDAY AT THE SEVENTH HOUR
by Jeanne Hale $1.50

The shocking news of the car accident—the doctor's verdict "massive brain-stem injury"—the despair of a mother's heartbreak. This is the tender story of the miraculous touch of God and the faith of a loving mother who believed Him with all her heart and saw her helpless teenage daughter restored to health and wholeness right before her eyes.

THERE'S DYNAMITE IN PRAISE
by Don Gossett $1.50

Here's how to get your prayers answered—and then some! Learn how, even in seemingly horrible circumstances, to unlock God's best for you—in a manual designed to lead you into a new and power-packed relationship with Him.

THE NEW WINE IS BETTER
by Robert Thom $1.50

A lively and often amusing account of Robert Thom's downward trek from a mansion in South Africa to the hopeless world of an alcoholic on the verge of suicide—and the whole new world of faith and power he discovered after Mrs. Webster came knocking on his door.

IF I CAN, YOU CAN
by Betty Lee Esses
$2.75

The wife of charismatic teacher Michael Esses tells how Jesus saved her husband and her marriage, and shares what He's been teaching the Esses ever since.

PLEASE MAKE ME CRY!
by Cookie Rodriguez
$1.75

The first female dope addict to "kick the habit" in Dave Wilkerson's ministry, Cookie was so hard that people said even death didn't want her. Told the way it really happened, this is the true story of how Cookie found Someone she wanted even more than heroin.

THE POWER OF THE BLOOD
by H. A. Maxwell Whyte
$1.50

A unique discussion of the power of the blood as well as practical instructions on how the blood of Christ may be used for a day by day victory over Satan.